URCELIA TEIXEIRA

A JORJA ROSE CHRISTIAN THRILLER

VALLEY OF DEATH SERIES BOOK 2 OF 3

SHADOW OF FEAR

SHADOW OF FEAR

A JORJA ROSE CHRISTIAN SUSPENSE THRILLER

VALLEY OF DEATH BOOK II

by URCELIA TEIXEIRA

Copyrighted material
E-book © ISBN: 978-1-928537-79-3
Paperback © ISBN: 978-1-928537-80-9
Independently Published by Urcelia Teixeira
First edition
Urcelia Teixeira, Wiltshire, UK
www.urcelia.com

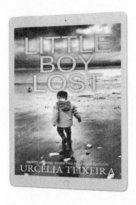

DEDICATION

To the women in my life
who stand fearless against the enemy,
who remain rooted in our shared faith,
who raise me up when I feel defeated,
who encourage me when I feel weary,
who lift me up in prayer when I am weak.
Thank you.

INSPIRED BY

"Yea, though I walk through the valley of the shadow of
death, I will fear no evil; For You are with me; Your rod and
Your staff, they comfort me."
Psalm 23:4
(NKJV)

CHAPTER ONE

RECAP - VENGEANCE IS MINE FINAL CHAPTER

J orja's feet dangled beneath her limp body as her mind slowly came back to life. Apart from the dull ache pounding against her brow, she felt little else.

She tried raising her head but could barely move. It felt leaden and unresponsive. The bloodied fluid that had pooled in the center of her bottom lip threatened to drop onto the floor and told her she was suspended, not lying down.

Turning her attention to the senses she had left, she heard nothing but silence at first. But, as her perception became more vivid, she was certain she was not alone. A scuffle to her right caught her attention, and she tried turning her head sideways to listen. There was shallow breathing directly beside her. Her mind instantly went to Ben, and she tried calling out his name. But the poison hadn't worn off yet, and it had left her tongue thick and bitter tasting. The vile sensation in her mouth made her feel sick, and she fought the urge to throw up. Desperate to make sense of it all, she willed her mind into full consciousness. Soon, fragments of memories cut through the blanket of fog that held her mind captive.

She recalled the sharp sting in her neck, Gustav's frantic shouting next to her, and Ben's muscular hand in hers. They'd been ambushed, taken by surprise, and driven to the ground without so much as a chance of fighting off Sokolov's men. Sobering thoughts drove through the fog. They were still alive. At least, she was.

"Ben," she forced his name from her numb lips, then listened.

Next to her, she heard him moan, barely audible, but she was certain it was him. She shot up a prayer of thanks that he was still alive and again called out to him. This time, his voice was louder. Still unable to lift her head much, she forced her heavy eyelids open. Her vision was blurry, but she soon traced the outlines of his body next to her. Like her, he was suspended from the roof; his hands bound high above his head.

Desperate to gain control of her body again, she tried moving her feet beneath her to support her weight. It worked, but her body weighed a ton and her injured arm suddenly shot immeasurable pain through her shoulder. They had tied her hands above her head too, unaware of the injury to her arm. Suddenly emotions overtook her and she tried to fight back the urge to cry, but couldn't.

Tears streamed down her cheeks. Tears of gratitude for being alive, but also tears of fear for the unknown. Sokolov could have easily killed them, yet he hadn't. Why? And where was Gustav?

With her sight now almost fully restored and the nerve-endings in her body slowly coming to life, she managed to lift her head off her chest. Next to her, Ben moaned as his body also steadily came to life.

"Ben, can you hear me?"

He moaned a response.

"You're okay, it's just the effects of the toxin still wearing off. Give it a few minutes."

The feeling in her legs had slowly returned and she managed to put her full body weight on her legs to stand. The motion instantly released the tension of the chains on her hands and arms.

Glimpses of clay-colored cobbles eventually flowed into a powdery amber floor. At first impression, it felt similar to that of a dank cellar of sorts, but it was far too expansive. There was something eerie about it, like death was present.

Gustav was nowhere to be seen and she looked over her shoulder searching for him. Loose chains similar to the ones that bound her and Ben were dangling close behind her and to her left. Fear suddenly gripped her. What if they had already killed him and they were coming for her or Ben next? She trembled at the thought of being tortured first. Sokolov had every reason to hold a grudge against her, and certainly against Gustav.

"Jorja, did they hurt you?"

Ben's voice had her turn to face him.

"No, I'm fine. You?" She noticed a deep cut above his nose and the dried blood on his skin.

"I'll live."

On his feet now too, he yanked at the chain above his head.

"It's no use. Save your energy."

She saw Ben searching the space.

"I think we're underground somewhere, maybe a cellar," she announced.

"Or a dungeon."

"They took Gustav. At least, I think they did. Look." She pushed her head back over her left shoulder to point out the shackles that dangled from the chain. "What if Sokolov tortured him to give back his money?"

"Then he got what he deserved."

"No one deserves death, Ben, no matter how much we despise him."

She bit her lip, forcing herself not to ask if he thought they'd come for her next. But Ben had sensed her burning question already.

"If he wanted us dead, his men would have killed us already."

She was about to offer her thoughts when the sound of keys clanked against a door somewhere in front of them.

They listened as an iron bolt scraped against metal before the door creaked open.

Feet shuffled toward them. As the faint light brought them into her vision, Jorja saw two burly men dragging Gustav toward them. When they were close enough and his face came into view, she saw he had been beaten. Her body tensed, steeling herself for what might become her fate next.

"What did you do to him? Why are we here?" she dared to ask.

The men ignored her questions and finished securing Gustav Züber to the chains. When they were done, they moved to one side, hands clasped in front of them like military men waiting for their next command.

Once more, footsteps announced the arrival of another captor, and they pinned their eyes onto the shadowy outlines of a well-dressed man as he slowly moved into the light.

Jorja recognized him the instant the light fell on his deep-set eyes that peered at her from beneath his heavy black brows. Artem Sokolov's angry gaze sliced into her soul, making her heart plunge to her stomach with dread.

She wanted to say something, but her tongue caught in her throat, and she tore her eyes away from his intense gaze instead.

He moved closer, so close that she could smell his expensive cologne, taste the vodka on his breath when he spoke.

"Your business partner is refusing to cooperate with me, Miss. Rose, so I am wondering what to do next."

"He's not my business partner," she replied, her tone icy.

Sokolov's eyes narrowed.

"I don't like liars, Jorja, especially if they lie to my face."

"She's not lying. Ben jumped to her defense.

"Tell your boyfriend to shut his mouth."

He let his unspoken threat linger before he spoke again. "Do you know why I had my men bring you here instead of killing you?"

She refused to answer.

"Fine, I will tell you. You and Mr. Züber cost me millions, not to mention the damage caused to my family name. So, I thought, I could turn a blind eye and let my men have the satisfaction of killing you, or I can do it myself. Naturally, you can understand that it will bring me much more pleasure to see you beg for your life before I kill you. So, here we are."

Sokolov turned to one of his men who handed him a gun before taking up his position again.

"But here is my problem. I don't know which one of you to kill first." He let out a sadistic laugh that echoed through the underground space.

Resting the tip of the gun against his dimpled chin, he looked at Gustav who was barely conscious. "Mr. Züber was my first choice because, well, it's obvious he ran the show and should therefore die first. Then again, I didn't expect to be lucky enough to also have your boyfriend join us."

"Leave him out of this, Sokolov. He had nothing to do with what happened," Jorja begged.

Sokolov laughed again.

"That is precisely my problem, Jorja. You see, to derive maximum satisfaction from this vengeful situation, killing him first will undoubtedly hurt you most. See where I'm going with this?"

His phone buzzed in his pocket and he stopped to read the text. Anger instantly flushed his cheeks and, seconds later, he dropped the phone back into his pocket. He took a few steps back then aimed his gun at Ben.

"Decision made. He goes first, then you, and finally Züber. Not only did the two of you steal from me, but now Züber's entire double-dealing business and client list is in every newspaper across the globe! Losing money is one thing, but taking my children's inheritance and tarnishing my family name is an entirely different situation."

He aimed the gun at Ben's chest, then turned to see the pain that Ben's death would render in Jorja's eyes.

"No, wait!" she yelled. "Let us go and I will not only get all your money back, but I will clear your name and ensure you have enough bargaining power to keep you out of jail for a very long time."

Sokolov's gaze probed her face but he held his aim, so Jorja tried to negotiate with him once more.

"I can get you the *Salvator Mundi*."

CHAPTER TWO

Silence fell as Jorja's words left her mouth and held Artem Sokolov's attention hostage. His dark eyes pierced her soul, searching, intruding, verifying her pledge.

"I can get you the *Salvator Mundi*," she repeated again, her voice slightly desperate as her eyes darted back and forth between Ben and the gun in Sokolov's hand.

"I heard you, Jorja. I just don't believe you." Sokolov called her bluff.

"It's the truth. I will get it for you if you let us go—all of us."

Something in Sokolov's eyes revealed that she had piqued his curiosity. She'd successfully hooked him, bought them some time.

But he wasn't budging.

Her heart pounded in her chest, her mind frantically

searching for what to say next that would clinch the deal toward their freedom.

"It's worth a lot of money, Artem. Half a million dollars by the most recent estimate, but it's worth a lot more to you in collateral."

She kept his gaze and waited for him to respond. Except he didn't. Instead, Gustav spoke.

"You're a traitor, Georgina." Gustav's strained voice rang in her ears as he spat a ball of bloodied saliva towards her. Sokolov laughed aloud at Gustav's unintentional confession before lowering the gun next to his side. "See, I knew you were hiding something, Züber. The two of you were planning a heist after all. And you said you weren't partners anymore." His tongue clicked against his teeth in disapproval as he moved to stand in front of Jorja.

"You surprise me, Jorja. I must confess. You had me for a moment. But that's what you are good at, isn't it? Being the mistress of deceit."

"We weren't planning anything, Artem. I didn't lie to you."

"She's a liar!" Gustav yelled out. "Everything she says is a lie."

His outburst had no effect on Sokolov, whose gaze continued to stare Jorja down. His eyes told her that he didn't believe her and as his hand lifted away from his side once more to point his gun at Ben's face, his cellphone rang.

The ringtone was that of a merry-go-round's and it

instantly snapped Sokolov's attention away from them. He dropped his aim and turned to take the call. When, a few moments later, his face revealed that the call must have been from one of his children, Jorja silently prayed it would have him leave the room. She needed more time to solidify her plan, to find out what Gustav knew.

When Sokolov ended the call, he handed his gun to one of his henchmen before facing his captives. Once more, his eyes were on Jorja.

"You must think me a fool, Jorja. The *Salvator Mundi* was purchased in a legal auction several years ago and I happen to know who bought it. I don't steal from my friends, not even to save my own skin."

He turned and swiftly left the room, his men following close behind him.

When the door closed behind Sokolov and his three prisoners were left alone, Gustav wasted no time.

"I should've known better than to get in bed with the likes of you again. You're an idiot, Georgina. You think you can bargain your way out of this, but you're dead wrong. Artem Sokolov will kill us the moment you hand over that painting."

"If you have a better idea to get us out of this mess alive, Gustav, then by all means, spit it out. I did what any normal human would do when a gun is pointed at her face."

"Yes, well, I guess it blew up in your face, didn't it? He'll be back and then he will finish us all off."

Jorja paused and ignored his bitter tirade. Her instincts were suddenly alive and she knew exactly why. "You don't know where it is, do you."

Gustav's expression revealed she had successfully guessed the truth.

"How did I not see that? You are the fraud you've always been, Gustav Züber! You don't have any idea where that painting is. Sokolov was right. It was sold via proxy at an auction and to this day, no one knows for certain who bought it or where it is. It's been missing for years. I cannot believe I fell for it."

Jorja looked away. Her insides were alive with fury. More than that, her body felt numb with fear.

She looked apologetically at Ben, whose warm eyes told her that everything would be okay. But she knew it wouldn't. She had made a promise she could not deliver on. A promise made in good faith trusting a sworn enemy who had nothing but malice toward her. They were going to die, all of them, down in the dungeons where their murders would be hidden from the world, their identities dissolved as if they'd never existed.

Near silent sobs pushed into her throat as she hung helplessly from the rafters above.

"You played me, Gustav. Our death will be on your head. This is all on you. You'll as much as pull the trigger yourself when he kills us. But the joke is on you, Gustav. During all our times together, you'd always told me how you wanted the world to remember you. The great Gustav

Züber. Art extraordinaire. Master appraiser. But you are nothing more than a lowly murderer, a liar. That's the legacy you'll be leaving behind. That's how the world will remember you. A cheating murderer." Her voice sounded dejected.

"I didn't play you, Georgina, and I'm not a murderer! I told you. I made many friends in prison and it just so happens that one of them is a member of a French mob. He told me the painting was hidden behind a wall somewhere in Abu Dhabi, and that he knew where."

"And let me guess. You promised him a cut when I stole it for you, didn't you?"

"Five percent. That's it. The rest is ours."

"Are you listening to yourself, Züber?" Ben spoke for the first time since Sokolov left. "You're talking as if there is still a deal on the table, trusting our lives in the hands of a French mobster's tip-off. That's if this mobster friend of yours is, in fact, even telling you the truth. Because, if he really knew where it was, then why not just steal it himself? You were duped, man, and now we're all going to die because of it."

"I wasn't *duped*. He had it on good authority. I trust him."

"Trust him? You're insane, Züber. The man's a gangster who will say anything you want to hear when you share a jail cell," Ben scoffed.

"It doesn't matter now anyway," Jorja said. "Who cares if your French mobster friend told the truth or not.

Sokolov has one up on us. Criminals like him are all in cahoots with one another. Heck, it might even be hidden behind one of his walls for all we know."

"The man told me the truth. Once you share a cell with an inmate there's a bond nothing can break. We stood together, had each other's backs. He's good for it."

"Like I said, Gustav, it doesn't matter. Sokolov isn't interested. We don't have any bargaining power without a worthwhile trade," Jorja reasoned.

"Oh, Artem Sokolov will come around. Just you wait and see. I've done enough business with him over the years to know what it looks like when a man has his back against the wall. You were right about one thing, Jorja. The *Salvator Mundi* was auctioned and bought by proxy, but it left the auction house and never made it to its destination. You, of all people, should know the bounty that would have been placed on that painting. I can think of at least a dozen very influential men who would have paid a small fortune to intercept that transfer. And as it happens, my guy worked for one of them."

Their conversation was interrupted when Sokolov re-entered the room. His facial expression looked noticeably different from when he had left earlier and Jorja spotted it immediately as he walked toward them. Under his heavy, dark eyebrows, his eyes took hers prisoner and lingered on her face. She tried to think of something to say but words escaped her. This was it. Their time was now.

Sensing what was to come, her eyes filled with tears and she looked sideways at Ben.

Each refusing to give Sokolov the satisfaction of seeing the pain in their eyes, Ben and Jorja held their gaze, resolute to face death's dark welcome together. In the hollow, cold underground space they heard Sokolov's finger pull back the hammer of his revolver, waited for the firing pin to slam against the cylinder that would discharge the first bullet, each expecting them to be first.

Gustav yelled, "No, please, stop!" But the thunderous clapping of the gunshot echoed through the space and instantly silenced Gustav's pleas.

Jorja's body shook uncontrollably when she realized Sokolov had shot and killed Gustav. Tears tightened her throat as she fought back the urge to explode into a sobbing mess. She will not give Sokolov the vengeful satisfaction he had been seeking, even if she choked to death on her fear.

Resolved in the knowledge that Ben would most probably be next, she shut her eyes and prayed that God forgave her for her part in it all, and that He would meet them both on the other side.

CHAPTER THREE

B elow her tear-soaked chin, the barrel of Sokolov's gun tilted Jorja's head up, forcing her to look at him. The metal was hot as it touched her skin, and even when he had succeeded in raising her head to face him, she kept her eyes shut.

"Look at me," Sokolov demanded between gritted teeth. His voice was cold and demanding.

Unable to defy him she opened her eyes and gasped when her eyes locked with his. In that moment, she knew she was no longer staring into the eyes of a mortal man. His eyes were black, glaring, piercing deep into the very essence of her being as if she had come face-to-face with the devil himself. Fear ran away with her and when she could no longer hold it back, it erupted in a wave of tears that lodged into her throat while he spoke.

"You have one week to get me that painting or he dies next."

The shock of his threat brought her tears to a dead halt. As he turned and barked a command at his men, Jorja yelled,

"I can't do it without Ben. I need him."

But her words had no effect on Sokolov, who continued walking towards the exit.

"Artem, please, there's no way I can pull a heist this big without Ben."

"A week, Jorja, or Ben joins your associate," Sokolov shouted over his shoulder before the door closed behind him.

HIS EVIL STARE LINGERED in her memory long after Artem Sokolov left the room and ordered his men to drop Jorja off in the center of town. Bound and blindfolded in the back of their car, she begged his men to persuade Sokolov to let Ben join her, but they ignored her and she eventually gave up asking.

They soon dumped her on the side of a steep embankment under a bridge, freed her sight and hands, then drove off. The night air was icy and wet against her skin as she lay there in the dark shadows of several tall trees. Her body felt sore and tender, her heart heavy with fear.

When she finally managed to pull herself up on her feet, she took in her surroundings and instantly recognized her location. Relief washed over her when she saw the Rhône River to her right. She was still in Geneva—the old city, to be precise.

The pain from her hurt arm was unbearable and she clutched it tightly against her body as she started to move up the small slope.

She'd need to find a place to stay, at least for the night, until she knew what to do next.

Exhausted, she shuffled across the cobbles of a nearby street as she followed the quiet road toward one of the smaller hotels she knew of. When she finally reached the unassuming boutique hotel, she stopped just outside the entrance, bending down on one knee as she buried her hand inside her sock. Moments later she retrieved a small bundle of cash, grateful that she'd kept up with the habit all these years.

'*Always come prepared*'. Ben's words echoed in her mind. It was one of the primary lessons he'd taught her back when they first started out together. She thumbed through the small wad of Sterling in her hand, counting out enough to pay for one or two nights' stay, and a little extra to motivate the clerk should he not accept foreign currency. Tucking the remainder back inside her sock, she rose to her feet and entered the building.

THE YOUNG MAN behind the front desk jumped to attention the moment the door chimes alerted him to her arrival.

"Bonsoir, Madame," he greeted.

"I need a room, please."

"But, of course, Madame. How many nights?"

"Two, for now, and it's not madame."

"Forgive me, Mademoiselle."

He continued with the reservation glancing suspiciously at the blood stains on her face and clothing.

"I had a car accident," she lied quickly, sliding several large notes across the desk.

The young desk clerk's eyes fixed on the cash which he quickly transferred to his pocket, aborting the formal reservation immediately after.

"I know a doctor if you need one."

"Thanks, but I just need a hot shower and a bed, and perhaps a bucket of ice, if possible," she added.

"Of course," he whispered as he pushed a room key across the counter and directed his eyes toward the stairwell.

"Second floor, turn right. It's the room at the end of the passage, nearest to the fire escape. I'll leave the ice and a few refreshments outside your door. Anything else, just dial nine from the room telephone. I'll be here all night." He finished with a polite smile.

She thanked the insightful clerk and made her way up the stairs and to her room.

Leaving the lights off, she drew open the heavy sunshine-yellow curtains just enough to allow the soft glow of the full moon in to partially light up the small room. Flinching in pain, she took off her leather jacket and tossed it onto the bed before she dropped down onto the edge of the bed next to it. For the first time in days, she was alone and out of danger, at least for the time being. It wasn't going to be easy, but she'd have to try and get a few hours of sleep. She was going to need it.

But, as her mind replayed the events that led up to that moment, alone in the dark hotel room, her emotions overwhelmed her.

Fear sat dormant inside the pit of her stomach, threatening to engulf her insides at any moment. For the first time in years, she felt completely helpless. In a brief moment of insanity, she thought of turning herself in to the police, seeking their help in finding Ben, telling them everything and bearing whatever dire consequences she had to face. But the thought quickly dissipated when Gustav's pleas rang in her head. Gustav was dead, killed in cold blood. If Sokolov could do that to him without as much as batting an eye, he would certainly kill Ben too.

Unless she gave him what he wanted.

But with Gustav now dead along with the name of the only lead she had to go on, it will be impossible to find the painting.

Her mind was frantic as she searched for a way out of the predicament she bluffed her way into. It wasn't supposed to go this way. Gustav wasn't meant to die. No one was supposed to die.

From the corner of her eye she glimpsed the red pocket-sized Bible on the nightstand and found herself leaning over to pick it up. The gold letters on the cover read, *Psalms and New Testament*, and she caught her heart flickering with sadness, as she recalled that the verse on the fridge magnet at home was from Psalms. Her fingers turned the flimsy pages to where she stopped at Psalm 23 before she read all six verses. By the time she neared the end she was sobbing uncontrollably. Just a short time ago she had finally yielded to God, confessed her sins, and asked Him to forgive her. Why did He not save her then, stopped all this from happening? Where were the green pastures and still waters He promised in these verses? Her eyes lingered on one particular verse, which she read over and over.

Even though I walk through the darkest valley,
I will fear no evil, for you are with me.

PUSHED to her feet by the insatiable turmoil that raged inside her soul, she walked over to the small en suite bathroom. The bright overhead light flickered on automatically as she entered, blinding her for a few quick moments. Once her eyes adjusted, she caught her reflection in the large mirror that stretched across the entire wall along the vanity. Her eyes were swollen from all the crying and her jawline bore a large purple bruise. And, as her gaze settled on the two-inch gash above her brow, she concluded that she was indeed in a valley. A deep, dark valley she had no idea how to get out of.

She freed a wayward strand of hair where it had gotten glued to the patch of dried blood around the wound. She looked a mess.

Questions flooded her mind as she tried to reason how it had come to this. Everything was fine until they had found her. How was it even possible that both Züber and Sokolov found her so easily? For two decades, she had kept a low profile and it had worked. She had been so careful, so where did she go wrong?

She stared at herself in the mirror for what seemed like hours, allowing her thoughts to run freely. A heavy blanket of guilt suddenly smothered her heart. Ewan would still be alive if she'd only trusted him. He had tried for years to get her to let him in. If only she'd let him. He would have found a way to protect her, to prevent all of this. What if she had let God in sooner too? Had she made her choice too late?

Her attention turned to Ben. He didn't deserve any of this either. None of this would have happened had she not contacted him. Now his life hung in the balance too.

She ran water over her face and hands before she stepped into the shower where she curled into a ball on the shower floor, desperate for the hot water to erase all that had happened.

CHAPTER FOUR

She'd fallen asleep with make-shift ice packs, made from the bucket of ice the desk clerk had left outside her door as promised the night before. She had wrapped it around her sore arm and it had melted, leaving the bedsheets soaked beneath her. The soothing moonlight had made way for a bright beam of sunshine that scattered the sense of new beginnings throughout the room. She jumped to her feet, putting her pants on in a hurry. Time was of the essence and she couldn't afford to waste any more. A heist of this nature would ordinarily take months of careful planning—with a skilled team. Instead, she had a week to pull it off entirely on her own.

As she put on her shoes, fear exploded into her heart once more. This time, however, her heart fought back.

"I will fear no evil, I will fear no evil," she repeated out loud.

She'd prayed herself to sleep the night before and decided to place her faith in God, even though she didn't fully know what that looked like yet. It was something she'd read on the cover of a book she'd recalled seeing on Ewan's kitchen table when she went over for tea once. Thinking back now, she wondered if that was one of the ways God had tried to get her attention.

Struggling to quiet the questions in her mind, she shoved them aside, hoping that the answers would soon become known to her. She needed to focus on the present.

Her fingers flipped through the few notes she had left. It wasn't nearly enough money for her to get the job done, and without her passport that Sokolov had held back, she had no access to her Swiss bank account either. Sticking the cash inside her pocket, she snatched her leather jacket off the bed next to her and slipped it on.

As she pushed herself up off the bed, a bright ray of sunshine hit her face and she found herself pausing to take it in, drawing a deep breath as if she wanted to inhale the unexpected lightness it brought to her soul. It was as if God Himself was holding her captive with the single beam of light that broke through the now cloudy sky outside her window. And in that moment, although her insides were tense with fear, her senses told her that she needed to do what she knew best and let God do what He did best.

The slightest of smiles curled from the corners of her mouth as she recalled a memory with Ewan. She had asked how he managed to stay true to his faith when he was forced to face evil people every day. He had answered that God always came through for him in every situation and that He'd never once let him down. That it was God's grace that allowed him to live in a world where evil drove people to do the things they didn't have the strength to deny. Through being given grace, he could in turn show grace.

"Show me grace, God, so I can show Sokolov grace too," she spoke into the beam of light.

THE OBLIGING CLERK from the night before had been replaced by a more mature woman who glared sideways at her when she passed the front desk. There was no doubt in Jorja's mind that the woman would scan the previous night's check-in list in search of her booking which, of course, didn't exist.

So, she ignored the woman, avoiding eye contact at all cost as she quickly slipped out the hotel's front door.

A bit further down on the opposite side of the street, she went inside a corner shop and bought a disposable cellphone, a takeaway coffee, and a kids pirate play set. Tucking the toy under one arm, her fingers dialed the number as soon as she stepped outside. Andre 'Mad Dog' Williams answered after just three rings.

"Yo."

"Andre, it's me."

"Gigi? Dang girl, what you go doing that for, huh?

Twice now you go ripping my heart out my chest. I thought you were dead for real this time."

His voice instantly lifted her spirits. To his cronies, he was simply Andre 'Mad Dog' Williams, the gangster in charge. But to her, he was the loyal friend she knew she could always rely on.

"I came close, but I'm okay. Sokolov got Züber though. He killed him."

Andre let out a gruff noise.

"Didn't I tell you not to mess with that man, huh? He's a level up on the danger scale, and it wouldn't surprise me if—"

"He has Ben," she cut in before he could rant about Sokolov being in the Russian mafia.

She could hear Andre punch into something as he groaned again.

"He's making you do something, ain't he?"

"I have one week to get him the *Salvator Mundi* or he kills Ben too."

Panic rang in Andre's voice when he spoke again.

"That's crazy, Gigi! A week isn't enough time to rob a small bank, never mind steal a famous painting, and that's if that dang thing even exists. If I remember correctly, it's been missing for years."

"I know. That's why I'm calling. I need your help, Andre."

"Wait! You mean you're actually going to do what he

wants. Steal the painting. That's insane, Gigi! Even for you!"

"I don't have much choice, do I? Enough blood's been shed and I'm not going to let Ben die too because of me. I have to do whatever it takes to get him out."

"And if you get caught? What good will it do then if you end up behind bars? Who's going to save Ben then, huh?"

"I have a plan. Besides, I can't think of that now. I have to at least try. I'm all he's got, Andre. Ben's life depends on me pulling this off."

"Don't be a fool, Gigi. The man is evil. Sokolov's not gonna let you or Ben go free once you get him what he wants. He'll kill you to protect himself and you know it."

Jorja had no words to refute him. She knew he was right. But then, she also knew she'd changed since they'd last seen each other.

Her silence made Andre speak again.

"I know a guy. He's dope it at these art things. He owes me a favor. We get him to do a fake and use that to get Ben back. He's good, Gigi, really good."

"It won't work. Artem Sokolov is no fool. He will have a top appraiser check the painting first, believe me."

Andre switched gears. "Where you at, fam?"

"Geneva."

"And Ben?"

"I don't know for sure. They blindfolded me when they took me away, but it's about fifteen minutes out of the city.

I'm to make contact once I have the painting. He kept my passport so I can't get any money from the bank."

"I'm on it. I'll text you a drop-off point. I'll have a new passport there before the sun rises tomorrow."

"Thanks, Andre, and I'll need one for Ben too, for when I get him out."

"Georgina, whatever you need, just say the word, okay? And watch your back."

"I will."

They ended the call and she swigged the last bit of coffee then dumped the empty container into the nearby garbage can. From the play set, she took the toy compass, buried it inside her pocket, and tossed the rest of the toys in the trash. The compass wasn't as good as the real thing, but it seemed to work when she'd quickly tested it. Pausing for a moment, she surveyed her surrounds, carefully searching for a mode of transportation. On the opposite side of the road, a few youths stood around chatting. Behind them, she spotted a couple of bicycles and a moped. Too slow and too much effort, she thought, and walked further along the road towards the center of the old town. It didn't take long before she spotted a faster motorcycle parked along one of the quieter side streets. *That'll do.* She smiled as she walked toward it.

With no one around it was an easy target and it took all of five seconds to bypass the ignition before she made away with the motorbike. A rush of energy flooded her body as the old familiar thrill of the game overtook her.

Then, as quickly as it came, guilt set in and she realized theft wasn't only against worldly laws, it was also against God's law. A law she was now desperate to follow. Conflict as to how her newfound beliefs could coexist with what she'd been forced into doing settled in the back of her mind. Would God forgive one more transgression if it meant she'd save Ben's life?

Her thoughts occupied her mind as she raced through the streets and set off toward Gustav's house.

CHAPTER FIVE

The hour flew by quickly and she relished the scenic drive along the lake to where the road eventually snaked between rows of tall trees before it ended at Gustav's house. She stopped under the trees several yards away, taking a moment to stake out what was left of the dwelling. It seemed quiet, so she approached with caution.

Across the grounds in front of the house, debris from the shootout still lay scattered all over the grass and deck. Bright yellow police tape spanned the front of the house and across the barely-there entrance. The door was charred and a thin film of soot covered the shattered windows and parts of the exterior walls. Recalling the fire-bomb Sokolov's men had thrown inside the house, she suddenly questioned if it was safe for her to enter, and if the secret passage she'd come there to find was still intact. She quickly brushed away the thought, concluding that, having known the way Gustav operated, he'd most likely have made certain the hideaway was built into a firewall.

Shards of glass crunched beneath her shoes as she entered the house. She moved quietly, her feet light as she stepped over pieces of burned furniture that were damaged by the fire and bullets. Chalked body outlines lay in wait along the way and she sidestepped them, feeling unsettled to be walking over them.

The house was silent, causing her every step to echo through the large space. From across the room, she spotted the wall that housed the hidden doorway and swiftly moved toward it. Remarkably, the fire hadn't touched the wallpaper and the hidden alcove had remained perfectly intact. When her fingers found the push-release latch of the hidden door, she paused, certain she had just heard footsteps walking over the scattered glass that lay inside the entrance of the house.

She froze and listened more intently. There it was again. Someone else was definitely inside the house. She stood in place, careful not to give away her position. Footsteps moved slowly across the scattered glass, deeper inside the house. As far as she could make out, it sounded like only one set, but there was no way of knowing for certain.

She thought of making her escape through the hidden door but recalled the elevator that was hidden behind it. The house was too quiet and the noise of it traveling down the shaft would undoubtedly give her position away in an instant. So, instead, she took cover around the corner of a nearby wall, waiting to catch a glimpse of whoever was snooping around in Gustav's house.

Or, had followed her there.

Armed with only her wit and a few rusty combat moves, every hair on Jorja's body stood on end as she waited for the intruder to make himself known. Her heart thumped loudly in her ears, but she held her position. The footsteps grew closer, paused, turned, then continued in her direction. She fell back against the wall behind her, pressed her head firmer against it. Her body was rigid, alert, ready to attack. The footsteps suddenly stopped mere feet away from her.

He had sensed her presence.

She held her breath, tuned her senses toward whoever was on the other side of the corner. Neither of them stirred as each waited for the other to make the first move. She held back the urge to play into his tactical maneuver, baiting him to doubt himself. It worked.

His feet shuffled ever so slightly on the floor as his weight shifted into a position of attack.

She was ready, pinning her sights on the bend where the two walls met.

With every sensory input in her body at its peak, the tip of his gun appeared from behind the wall, slowly revealing the imminent danger behind it, one inch at a time.

She barely breathed, waiting for him to move forward a bit more.

He did and she seized the moment.

Her hand closed around his wrist, using it to thrust his arm back into the edge of the wall.

He fought back and came at her with his free arm.

She blocked his punch, pounded his armed hand harder against the wall until the weapon fell to the floor between them.

His body thrust toward her, spinning her around, then pinning her back against the wall, holding her in place with his strong forearm across her neck. The black mask on his face revealed nothing but his eyes. Hazel eyes under thick, blond brows. She fought back against his strength and tried pushing her weight against his. Her strength surprised him, evident also by the soft groans that now escaped from beneath his strained breath that puffed out the thin fabric over his mouth.

She freed an arm and curled her hand toward the back of his head in an attempt to yank the mask from his face.

But he was too quick and stopped her from doing it, gripping her wrist harder and pinning her arm against the wall above her head.

Still in his overpowering grip, he left her no choice and she did what any woman in her position would do: she thrust her knee into his groin.

The power move had the desired effect and instantly

forced him to release the grip from her neck. He doubled over, panted for air.

Once more, she used her knee and delivered a forceful blow to his face. He fell back onto his spine, spitting a few words in French at her as he fought to catch his breath.

She turned around to find his gun on the floor behind her but when she spun back around to aim it at him, he had already bolted for the exit.

"Stop!" she shouted and ran after him.

He ignored her and kept running until he made it outside and onto the front of the house.

"I said, stop! Who are you? What do you want?"

She followed him down to the water's edge but he was too fast and jumped aboard a speedboat that lay in wait for him. No wonder she hadn't heard him coming, she thought, as she reached the water. The masked man mockingly saluted her as he joined an accomplice before they sped off across the water, as if to say he'd be seeing her again. It puzzled her. How did they know she was there? They had arrived in a boat, which meant they couldn't have followed her by road.

Tucking the gun inside her waistband in the small of her back, she walked back up to the house, her mind racing through the chain of events. Then it dawned on her. Perhaps they hadn't come there for her after all. Perhaps she had surprised them instead. And if that were the case, what were they looking for?

She paused, her thoughts once she reached the hidden

passage. She'd figure it all out later. For now, she needed to stay focused and on track.

THE DOOR RELEASED QUICKLY, just as she recalled seeing it doing when Gustav did it. As before, the elevator took her underground and stopped once it delivered her to the subterranean tunnel. Retrieving the cheap compass from her pocket, she stepped forward, counting each pace she made, taking note of the changes in direction each time. Fifty-three paces south, then ninety-seven south-west, and so on, until she reached the end of the tunnel where Gustav's pupils would be needed to unlock the retina scanner to open the exit door. With it being what she had already anticipated, she made sure she had logged the map points in an unsent text message on her phone, using the phone as a notebook instead.

Satisfied her tracking method would work above ground, she headed back along the hidden tunnel, up the elevator and out into the house. Her hand went to the small of her back where she had placed the gun she'd seized from her attacker earlier. Firming her clasp around the grip, she re-entered the home. When she found no evidence of a threat, she relaxed then took note of the elevator's positioning in relation to the space outside the house. Feeling as if danger was imminent, she moved quickly, exiting the rear of the house where she'd be better aligned to follow her make-shift map. Counting the paces, she tracked the direction with her toy compass, which now proved to be unaligned with the actual polar orientation points.

She tapped her finger at the glass, but the needle remained in place. It didn't matter if south was true south or not. As long as she followed the compass bearings, she should be fine, she assured herself.

CHAPTER SIX

C onscious of her attacker returning to finish what he'd started, she navigated the terrain with ease until the woods behind the house grew so dense that it made counting her paces much harder. Several times she slipped on large exposed roots, once nearly twisting her ankle in the process. She told herself to go at it slower, to not let the time crunch faze her too much. But all she could think about was Ben, locked up in that dank underground space by a vicious murderer. She forced her mind back to the task at hand, reminding herself that losing count would only delay matters further.

It took nearly two hours through the thick forest before her tracking maneuver delivered her to a dirt road that snaked between the tall trees. Rotating in all directions in search of Gustav's secret hideaway, she found nothing but more trees. Annoyed with herself for allowing herself to get distracted and messing up, she cursed herself.

"Stupid woman! What were you thinking?"

Frustration soon made space for fear and she collapsed onto her knees, fighting hard not to lose total control of the situation. *God, if you can hear me, help me, please? I can't let him die too.*

She sat there on the ground, her legs folded beneath her body, desperate to take charge of her raging emotions and remedy the helpless situation she now found herself in. Drawing a few deep breaths, she shook her head as if to shake all the negativity from her mind and off her shoulders.

"You can do this, Jorja. It's okay. Just keep going," she spoke encouraging words to herself and wiped at the droplets of sweat that had mixed with her tears.

Back on her feet, she looked over at the spot between the trees where she'd left the forest then, walked back to it. Checking the notes on her phone she tried to orient herself. Once again, she tapped her finger on the glass of the compass and saw the wonky needle change direction twice before it swung back to its original direction. She walked back out onto the road and decided to take a chance by picking one of the directions. She glanced up at the sun, taking note of its polarity and decided to turn west when she suddenly recalled a silly rhyme she once had to say in a school play. *'West is best when you go on a quest. East leads to strangers that spell nothing but danger.'*

"West it is, then," she decided.

The road was straight, slightly overgrown, and just wide enough to allow a single vehicle through. As far as she could see, there were no tracks in the sandy bed to indicate any recent activity on the road. That was a good thing, she thought, since it supported her hope that it was a private road that might, by some miracle, lead to Gustav's hideout. Concluding that her bearings couldn't have been too far off, she continued.

Hope filled her and made her step lighter. But as she neared the half hour count along the road, doubt settled in. When she was once again moments away from giving up, she spotted the entrance of a barely visible path that turned up between the trees. She ran toward it, suddenly not thinking twice to follow the uneven turf that was nearly entirely covered by overhanging foliage that flanked its sides. The crooked footpath ran along an upward slope before it suddenly stopped outside a wrought-iron gate. Similar in size and shape to that of a door, its hinges were busted on both sides where it had once been bolted into the wall. Made of unevenly shaped stones that looked like they might have been there forever, the wall was overgrown with moss, blending seamlessly with the foliage surrounding it.

Her heart skipped several beats as she pushed her way through the broken gate, concluding that it must have been how Sokolov's men had entered Gustav's property to ambush them on the other end of the tunnel. This was it.

She had found Gustav's hidden fortress and God had helped her—she was certain of it.

THE SPEEDBOAT RACED across Lake Geneva until it reached its destination a quarter of a mile south. The two men hurriedly tied its ropes to the mooring then made their way up the jetty toward the house. Speaking French, they argued with one another, each blaming the other for failing their mission.

Anxious about having to deliver a report to their employer, they made their way past the two armed men who were posted at the front entrance of the stately lakeside house. When they entered the private study to face their fate, fear lay deep in the etchings of their faces.

"I assume you acquired it." The sophisticated female voice came from behind the antique desk where she was seated in a large red button-leather chair, its back turned toward the two men.

"No, madame, it was nowhere to be seen."

The chair slowly swung around and they were greeted with their commander's cold stare.

"We ran into some trouble, madame." The other man quickly continued the report, intentionally withholding that they were scared away by someone of the opposite sex.

The woman's bright red lips pouted before her bejeweled fingers with matching red fingernails brought a slim cigarette to her mouth. She drew in the tobacco and slowly puffed a strong cinnamon scented cloud into the air above her head.

"So you failed," she said, her voice bearing almost no emotion before she reached to pick up her cup of espresso.

"We'll find it, Madame Bouvier."

She threw her head of thick, pitch-black hair back as she bellowed a sarcastic laugh. But her forced smile soon transformed into the same cold stare they were greeted with.

"You failed." Her black-lined eyes were angry from beneath her blunt bangs that lightly touched her long eyelashes every time she blinked.

She killed the cigarette and immediately drew a new one from the chocolate-colored Davidoff cigarettes pack on her desk before the man to her left leaned in to light it for her. Up until now, the man had stood to one side, looking out the window, his back facing the room. Well-groomed in an expensive gray suit, he was tall, dark, and dashingly handsome, the type of man Madame Bouvier enjoyed being seen with. As soon as he lit her cigarette, he turned away and continued staring out the window behind her.

"Madame, we looked everywhere. The house is in ruins; there was nothing there. Züber must have it somewhere else."

She launched to her feet. "You imbeciles! Gustav Züber is dead. His body was found early this morning under the bridge by the river. All the pair of you had to do was find out where he kept my painting. Simple, yet you failed miserably. Do you have any idea what that painting is worth to me—to my family? It has been in my family since Da Vinci painted it! Züber was the only man on this planet who gave us any chance of getting it back on these walls where it belongs. You were in his house, the very place he lived and worked, and you're telling me you couldn't find a single piece of paper bearing a name or an address."

"Like we said, madame, the house was destroyed."

Madame Bouvier flicked her long black hair behind her shoulders before she sat back down in her chair. "My father would turn in his grave if he knew you had failed him. If he were still alive, I am very certain he would have fired you on the spot."

"Yes, madame," the men answered in unison.

"I suggest you go back to the house and keep looking until you find something that will tell me where he kept that painting. If Züber had it, and I believe he did, it's around here somewhere." She looked over her shoulder to the man at the window. "Isn't that right?"

The man twisted the upper half of his body and spoke over his shoulder, his hands neatly placed behind his back. "I would agree with you, Gabrielle. In my experience, it is very difficult moving a painting of that magnitude out of any country. In our last meeting with Mr. Züber, he had indicated that the painting was within easy reach, so I am assuming he had it in his possession, or at the very least, somewhere here in Geneva."

Madame Bouvier clasped her tanned fingers atop her desk, raising her gaze toward her two henchmen.

"No more excuses. Go back to his house and find me something, anything. You might have been in my father's employ a long time, but know this: if you come back empty-handed again, you're going home to your wives with nothing but this month's paycheck. Do I make myself clear?"

"Yes, madame, and the woman, what shall we do with her?" The driver of the boat dared to ask, prompting a questioning sideways glance from his betrayed accomplice.

From beneath her thick, black bangs, their employer raised an eyebrow, soon followed by a similar curious look from the man by the window.

"What woman?" Madame Bouvier asked.

CHAPTER SEVEN

Alone in Gustav's safe house, Jorja took her time rummaging through the drawers of the desk in his study. Her eyes danced between ledgers and appraisal documents, finding nothing to make known the location of the *Salvator Mundi*. Frustrated, she scooped an arm behind a row of books on the nearby bookshelf, throwing it in a messy pile to the floor.

"Come on, Gustav, where would you hide the file? I know it's here somewhere. You were always so meticulous with the details of your projects, so where did you hide the file on this one?" She spoke as if he was in the room with her, as if he'd answer her.

With her hands on her hips, she stood in the center of the room, scanning it in search of anything she might have missed. But there was nothing there.

A hollow feeling of dread pushed into her heart and

made it skip a beat before it sank like a pile of stones in her stomach. Gustav was a con artist, a fraud who tricked buyers into paying huge sums of money for forgeries or, worse, stolen paintings, often inflating the prices along the way. He'd pinned anonymous buyers against each other, auctioning the paintings to the highest bidder before he sank his grubby paws into the winner. Nothing was beneath him and he was as devious and slick as a slithering snake lying in wait for his next prey. Twenty years ago, they had stood on the same side of the moral fence and he had no reason to hide anything from her. But everything had changed, and though he had revealed his plans, she was the one person he hated most in the world. And, she was now convinced, he had conned her too.

If he were alive, she would shake the truth out of his timid body. But, he wasn't. He had died at the hands of the man she feared more than a thousand deaths. A man whose eyes were as dark as his soul. A man who had promised to take hers.

And he had Ben.

She buried her face in her palms, rubbing her hands vigorously over her face before she smoothed them back over her hair.

"You can do this, Jorja, you have to, for Ben's sake. Think...think!"

Chewing at the soft flesh inside her bottom lip, she decided to search Gustav's bedroom. He'd been in jail and it was said that ex convicts' world of reference shrunk when they returned to life after prison. If that fact rang true, he might have hidden the details somewhere in his room, where he'd become accustomed to feeling safe.

She ran up the staircase to the second floor, taking the steps two at a time. Several large paintings decorated the wall alongside it. Nothing of great value—as far as she could tell.

But, in his bedroom, she quickly froze where she'd stopped at the foot of his bed. Suddenly more questions than she had time to digest flooded her mind. There, on the wall above his bed, evenly spaced in two neat rows of six, hung twelve small paintings. Her breath caught in her throat, as if someone had just punched the air out of her stomach. Jorja stared at Claude Monet's entire collection of Charing Cross Bridge paintings, including the five unique replicas she'd acquired for Myles Brentwood.

Stunned, she walked around the bed to get a closer look. Certain that her eyes were deceiving her, she climbed atop the bed, leaning closer to study the replica artist's distinct signature strokes. She had studied them all too well. There was no mistaking it. The paintings hanging above Gustav's bed, displayed like trophies for his secret pleasure, were the ones that had gone missing from Myles' house, hours after he'd been at her shop to collect his final purchase.

Jumping off, she paced the length of the bed, desperate to make sense of it all. How had Gustav come to have these paintings? Did he kill Myles? And Ewan! Had it been him behind their murders all along? Or were he and Sokolov working together? Nothing made sense anymore and she thought of calling Charlie to tell him she'd found the paintings they'd been looking for—and Myles' murderer.

But she shelved the prospect as soon as her rational thoughts resurfaced. She couldn't call Charlie, not now. She had disappeared into thin air over a week ago. He would ask too many questions. Questions she couldn't explain without telling him who she really was—or what she'd gotten herself entangled in. And Charlie, being the stickling law keeper he was, would not walk away until he put Sokolov behind bars. That would jeopardize everything—and quite possibly get Ben killed in the process. No, she finally decided, she couldn't risk it. Besides, it wouldn't make any difference now anyway. Gustav was dead. So were Myles and Ewan.

She turned to look at the paintings once more. Like she needed to reassure herself that she wasn't imagining it. Sick to her stomach, she tore herself away from what she had just discovered. None of this changed anything, except that she now knew Gustav got what he deserved. He was no different than Sokolov. They were one and the same. Cold-blooded murderers who harbored more secrets than she cared to know.

Forcing herself into the present, she searched through his bedside tables, now more determined than ever to find what she came there for so she could put this entire horrific ordeal behind her.

But the contents delivered nothing but a few small personal items, not even a flash drive. She stuck her hand deeper inside the cherrywood drawer, feeling her way through a few loose coins, a couple of pens, and an antique pocket watch. As she pulled the watch out, the gold chain snagged on a small piece of bright orange fabric that, at first instinct, she tried pulling off, fully intent on tossing it back into the drawer.

Until her mind made sense of what it was: a prison number.

Dropping the watch back inside the drawer, her attention turned to the piece of fabric she now held in her hand. It had been cut from a piece of clothing, the uneven edges giving away that it might have been done with something other than a pair of scissors. Perhaps it was Gustav's prison number, kept as a souvenir.

But what if it wasn't? What if the fabric belonged to his cellmate, the very acquaintance he so proudly boasted had tipped him off on the whereabouts of the *Salvator Mundi*?

As she stood there fingering the fabric, trying to make sense of the riddles that swirled in her head, a thought snapped into place. There was no file because he hadn't made one yet. All he had was the so-called tip-off from his fellow inmate. A tip he must have only just received. That's why he had come for her. He needed her, and Ben, to do his dirty work for him, to find the painting, to build his file.

Which meant only one thing: she had to find Gustav's prison roommate and make him tell her what he knew.

Finding the French gang member was her only chance at finding out exactly where the painting was—if it even still existed.

With her heart now pulsing excitedly in her chest, she set off to the den where she had found Gustav's computer earlier. She sat down in front of it, fighting the anxiety that teased at her insides when booting it up took longer than she had anticipated. When the screen eventually lit up, she clicked the cursor across the screen, searching for any information she could find which might indicate who his cellmate was or, more importantly, where she could find him.

His email inbox revealed a few letters from the prison board. She scanned through the contents and easily found Gustav's prison number in the top corner on one of the letters. Holding the piece of orange fabric up to the number on the screen, she compared the two numbers.

They weren't a match.

Thrilled with her discovery she safely assumed that it must then belong to his cellmate. Odd as it might be for Gustav to have held onto it, she was certain of her suspicions. If only she had a way of finding his name, where he lived and if he was still in prison, or if he too had been released. If only she had Ben, who she knew would've already found his way into the prison's database to reveal the information.

She skimmed a few more emails, desperate to find what she needed, before she once more settled on the name of Gustav's parole officer, noted at the bottom of the parole board letter. She copied his contact details onto a sticky note and slipped it inside her pocket.

Without Ben's help there was only one way to track down Gustav's fellow inmate, and it might not be as easy a task as she was hoping for.

CHAPTER EIGHT

A s always, Pascale Lupin parked his car two blocks away from the restaurant. The crisp evening air hit his body when he stepped out, causing him to flip the collar of his black cashmere coat over his neck. From there, it was a quick walk to his destination along the banks of the Rhône then up past the church. After five years, he knew the route well—every cobble and every pothole in the road.

As always, he stayed vigilant, sneaking glances behind him every few yards along the way. It's what was necessary in his line of business if he wanted to stay alive.

When he eventually reached the restaurant, he paused a few shops away, leaning against a lamp post to light his Gauloises. As he dragged on the cigarette, he staked out the surroundings—another precautionary habit he'd picked up over the years. Satisfied there were no noticeable threats, he inhaled three quick draws of his cigarette, stubbed it under his expensive Italian leather shoes, and crossed the street toward the restaurant.

To the ordinary man on the street, La Petite Maison was one of the top French restaurants in Geneva, and unlike the name suggested, was not the cosy, little house everyone thought it was. Crisp white damask tablecloths, crystal wine glasses, and Michelin star French food was nothing but smoke and mirrors to what truly happened within those walls. For behind the facade, one floor below ground, one of Europe's oldest and most dangerous organized crime syndicates gathered to strategize over all things illicit.

Pascale had first met its ringleader, Gerard Dubois, six years ago at an exclusive VIP art auction sponsored by his good friend, Jacques Bouvier. He had impressed both men with his unsurpassed technical knowledge of some of the world's most famous artists, and was soon recruited into the Bouvier organization. Gerard Dubois and Jacques Bouvier's friendship stretched over several decades to when both of them had first moved to Switzerland as teenagers, attending the same elite school in Geneva. But unlike Bouvier, his friend, Dubois, chose to make his name and fortune by means of participating in high profile illegal endeavors, soon affording him significant power and criminal status across Europe.

When early on in Bouvier's career, a foolish night of partying led to an accidental hit and run that threatened to jeopardize his marriage and career, Dubois used his influence to buy his friend's freedom. But it wasn't until much later that Bouvier realized the simple favor had cost him far more than he had realized and that their friendship would take on an entirely different meaning in the years to come when Gerard Dubois used his friend's guilt and past mistake to further his own gain. Forever indebted to Dubois for keeping him out of prison and saving his life, Jacques Bouvier played a pivotal role in his friend's illegal operations, using his auction house to fence the art pieces Dubois had illegally acquired. Jacques Bouvier had been trapped in a web of lies until the day he died.

But, it wasn't long before Bouvier's daughter fell in love with Pascale's charisma, and the two entered into a relationship that had Pascale securely rooted in the Bouvier empire by the time her father died. And, unaware of her esteemed father's significant interests in the Dubois organization, Gabrielle Bouvier became the perfect pawn that placed Gerard Dubois in the prime position he needed to be in order to continue his clandestine business activities.

So, when Jacques Bouvier died, taking his secrets to his grave, his sins continued long beyond his death and Pascale became Gerard's much needed man on the inside.

"Good evening, Monsieur Lupin," the friendly restaurant hostess said as he entered.

He tipped his head and smiled as he passed her, making his way to the door in the far corner of the restaurant.

The two muscly men who stood on guard in front of the door stepped aside and let him through. They had come to know him over the years and treated him with the utmost respect, knowing full well how important his relationship with their employer was.

The familiar staircase took him to the restaurant's basement where a short, narrow corridor led him through large wooden doors and into the Dubois headquarters. Exquisitely decorated with luxurious antique furniture and rich red colors, it looked like an exclusive private gentlemen's club fit for aristocracy, complete with a butler standing on call to the side. In the farthest corner, Gerard Dubois sat reading his newspaper in a vintage ox-blood leather wingback chair, his beefy fingers curled around a thick Cuban cigar.

Peering over the edge of his newspaper, his face lit up as soon as Pascale entered.

"Just the man I was hoping would save me from the pestilent news they call good reporting. When are these people going to give us something a bit more meaty to sink our teeth into?"

He dropped his paper on the nearby table and beckoned Pascale to take a seat opposite him.

"And by 'meaty' I take it you mean something that would grab your interest, like, I don't know, the discovery of an ancient painting that's worth millions, perhaps?"

Gerard gave a throaty chuckle from beneath a cloud of cigar smoke. "You know me too well, Pascale."

And he did. Pascale had long since established Gerard possessed a huge lust for high ticket art. Partly because he knew the true currency of these items, and partly because his ego loved the challenge.

"So, what brings you here, my friend? Tell me you have something interesting for me, something to bring back some luster to my life."

Pascale settled into the chair opposite his employer. "I think I just might, yes."

"I'm intrigued."

"I take it you've already heard that they found Gustav Züber's body this morning."

"Indeed I have. The deadbeat fraud finally got what was coming his way."

"Might be, but... " Pascale paused for effect.

"Spit it out, man," Gerard said impatiently as he shuffled to the edge of his seat.

"Gabrielle and I suspect the guy might have actually been onto something."

Gerard shuffled back into his chair and crossed his arms as he rolled his eyes, dismissing what he already suspected was going to come from Pascal's lips.

"Oh, not this ridiculous nonsense about the *Salvator Mundi* again. Surely you of all people know better, Pascale."

"I think the guy was telling the truth, Gerard."

"I've known Züber a long time, Pascale, and believe me when I tell you he was a master at conning vulnerable women out of their family fortunes. It was no secret that Jacques' dying wish was for his daughter to get that painting back under Bouvier ownership. Züber saw an opportunity and did what every low-life conman would do to a daughter grieving the death of her beloved father. He preyed on Gabrielle's vulnerability, played her, told her what she was desperate to hear. She's a fool if she thinks he was telling the truth. Take it from me."

"Ordinarily, I would believe you, Gerard, but not this time. She sent two investigators to Züber's house to look for the painting."

"Let me guess. They didn't find it."

"Right, but there was someone else snooping around in the house. A woman."

Gerard burst into laughter. "The man was in jail for years, Pascale. It wouldn't be the first time an ex con kept some company."

"Oh, she wasn't company, I assure you. From what the men said, she was no weak damsel. She packed a serious punch."

Gerard sat forward in his chair again. "Any idea who she is?"

"Not yet, but I have a few people looking into it."

Gerard's eyes narrowed as he studied Pascale's face, his mouth sucking on his cigar a few times before he spoke again.

"You really think he knew where the Da Vinci is."

"I do."

"And you suspect this mysterious woman is after it too."

"I do, yes."

"Except, of course, the weasel is now dead and he's taken its location to the pits of Hell. How typical of him."

"Perhaps not all is lost, Gerard. When he initially came to the house to meet with Gabrielle, he had mentioned that he'd received a tip-off on where the painting is. As I recall, he'd said the tip came from his former cellmate, some French mobster, if I'm not mistaken."

Gerard called his butler over then asked that he hand him his mobile phone. "I'll take care of it. He'll be easy to find. In the meantime, find this mystery woman and find out what she knows. If she's after the painting, we can simply throw a bit of money at her and book her a one-way ticket to a tropical island somewhere. It wouldn't surprise me if she's just one of Züber's scorned victims of deceit coming to claim a bit of whatever his lying mouth had promised her."

Pascale jumped to his feet. "I'm on it. I'll keep you posted."

As he bid his farewell and started toward the exit, Gerard called out after him. "Job well done, Pascale, and if the *Salvator Mundi* is out there, I want it. I don't care what it takes."

CHAPTER NINE

The address in her pocket led Jorja to a busy neighborhood on the other side of the city. As she stood in the shadows to one side, carefully watching the frontage of the block of apartments, she finished the fresh pretzel she'd bought from one of the street vendors a few blocks away. Standing there, watching the entrance, reminded her of the times she'd done a stakeout of their next heist—observing and studying their target to ensure their plan was airtight. The memory stung, because this time Ben wasn't in her ear as backup, nor would he be there when she would need to execute this heist. She shoved the feeling aside, focusing her attention back to the moment at hand.

Across the street, the apartment building's entrance remained closed, secured in place by an electronic lock.

One she'd ordinarily bypass with ease if she had her bag of equipment on her. For now, she'd have to fall back on more primitive measures.

It was already dark and close to dinner time, which meant it won't be too long before takeout deliveries would present the opportune time for her to sneak in with an unsuspecting delivery guy.

It took hardly any time at all before the first delivery car pulled up in front of the building, and she quickly made her way across the street. Beating the youngster to the door, she pretended to be preoccupied on her phone, letting him go ahead of her when his client buzzed him in before she sneaked in behind him. Four flights of stairs later, she stood outside the door that belonged to Gustav's parole officer. With the hallways clear on both sides, she curled her hand around the grip of her gun, keeping it hidden in the small of her back.

She knocked twice, called out, "Delivery for Bernárd," then waited, her head bowed.

From the other side of the door she heard shuffling, then a pause as the man looked through the peephole.

"I didn't order anything," his voice came back.

"This is apartment four twenty-six, is it not?"

"Yes, but—"

"And you are Bernárd de La Fontaine, are you not?"

"Yes."

"Then you have a delivery. I need you to sign, please?"

She heard the door chain drop before his hand moved over the lock to open the door. The instant the door opened, Jorja threw her full weight onto the door, pushing Bernárd to the ground as she forced her way inside his apartment. Before he had a chance to fight her off, she had already shut the door behind them and pinned him to the wall with her gun aimed at his chest.

"Give me what I need and you won't get hurt," she said calmly.

"You can take my wallet, there, on the table. Take anything," Bernárd said.

"I'm not here to rob you. I need a name."

"Fine, whatever you need," he agreed.

"I need the name and address of the man who shared a prison cell with Gustav Züber."

"How should I know who his cellmate was? I was his parole officer, not his prison guard."

"Get up," Jorja commanded, then pointed the gun toward his face.

Bernárd did as he was told. "Who are you, and why do you want his name?" he bravely asked.

"It doesn't matter. Just do as you're told and you won't die."

Once again, he did as she instructed.

"Where's your computer? I know you have access to the database, so get cracking. The quicker you give me the information, the quicker I leave."

He jutted his chin out toward the cross-shoulder laptop bag that rested on the floor next to a lime green sofa in the next room.

"Get it, slowly."

The man moved to pick up the bag, then, as he stood up, swung the bag back, intending to hit the gun from her hand. But his maneuver was too slow for Jorja whose experience had already prepared her for it and, with her other hand, she caught onto the bag's strap and twisted it around the man's hand. As she did so, she thrust her heel into the back of his knee while bending his arm flush against his back. As he hunched forward in pain, she planted his face firmly into the lime green cushions.

The man groaned as his head hit the sofa.

"I warned you not to do anything stupid. Try that again and you'll end up with a broken arm. Got it?"

He nodded.

"Now, open it up and get me that name and address."

WHEN BERNÁRD eventually handed the cellmate's information to her, she used the back of her gun to render him unconscious, stuffed a sock inside his mouth and hogtied his hands and feet before locking him inside his bathroom. Shutting the apartment door behind her, she struggled to contain the wretched feeling that seemed as if her insides had ignited and threatened to burn her alive. Once outside, she ran as far away from the building as she could, desperate to rid her body from whatever evil was inside her. When she finally stopped at the edge of a small public play area, tears were already running down her face. She hated every moment of what she'd just done. It wasn't who she was anymore and having to force herself to become that hateful person made her sick to the stomach.

Hunched over with her hands on her knees, she retched in the nearby bushes, her body convulsing as if she tried to rid it from the evil she now felt was slowly sneaking back into her life.

And there was no stopping it.

In the quiet corner of the playground, she fell on her knees and lifted her eyes to the starry night above. *I can't do this, God. Don't make me do this, please.* Her prayerful pleas echoed inside her heart, aching as she begged with God to save her from herself. But, deep down, she already knew that there was no other way and that it was what was necessary if she were to save Ben's life.

As the tears slowly faded, and her thoughts became clearer, she looked at the piece of paper Bernárd had given her. She had the name and address she needed but below that, he had written 'Burn in Hell!' in big, bold letters. The cursing words stung. She was nothing like Sokolov and Gustav. She wasn't evil, not anymore. If only he knew she was on his side of the law. If only he knew why she was doing this.

With numb fingers she tore the words away from the address and scrunched the paper into a small ball before tossing it into the bushes. Her mobile buzzed inside her pocket, forcing her attention away from the self-pity that had suddenly overwhelmed her with fear. Wiping her face with the back of her hand, she read the message. It was Andre, sending the details of where she would find her passport: St Pierre's Cathedral, left aisle, eighth pew from the front. The time stated 10 p.m. She texted him back to thank him then checked the time on her watch. She had less than an hour to get to the church. The inmate would have to wait for now. Not only was the address located in another city, she also sensed getting him to talk might not be as easy as she was hoping it would be. And with Bernárd knocked out and tied up, it was safe to say he wouldn't manage to free himself in time to warn the guy she was coming for him. Besides, the mere thought of going to a church instead was far more appealing and, as relief washed over her and her heart overruled her mind, her insides instantly warmed to the sudden change of plans. It was precisely the thing she needed now most. A time to soak in God's presence, to seek His forgiveness once again, and to draw new strength to continue with her mission.

OUT OF MONEY and without transport, the walk took longer than she had hoped it would. Along the way she had contemplated stealing a car, but couldn't bring herself to do it. She had already decided that she would only do what was absolutely necessary to complete her mission. Nothing more and nothing less, just enough to do what needed to be done to save Ben from Satan's clutches—and help her keep her soul.

By the time she reached the banks of the river, her feet ached. In the distance, she heard the first church bell echo into the darkness, marking the time as ten o'clock. She stepped up her pace, navigating the uneven cobbled stones with difficulty, nearly twisting her ankle twice in her haste. Anxious that she'd miss the meet-up, she settled into a light jog and ran faster toward the street that would take her to the church. As she rounded the corner, her body took on a momentum of its own. Unable to stop in time, she crashed into a man, his body hard as steel against hers. The impact thrust her back and pushed her off her feet, delivering her with a thud onto the ground in front of him. With one eye on the church tower's clock, she peeled herself off the ground, accepting the stranger's hand to help her to her feet. Her hand easily disappeared into his and she noticed the small tattoo inside his wrist when his black cashmere sleeve pulled away just enough to reveal it.

"I am so sorry, madame," his warm voice brought her eyes to his. "Are you hurt?"

His face was friendly, and she found herself almost fully mesmerized by his strikingly handsome features. Behind him, the last bell chimed and she caught herself having to force herself to let go of his hand. Ignoring his questions, she rushed toward the church without answering or looking back. From behind, she heard the man call out to her again, asking if she was okay, apologizing for bumping into her. But she brushed it off and ran up the large steps before disappearing behind the heavy wood-carved doors of the church.

CHAPTER TEN

The church was as soothing to her soul as she had ached for it to be and the soft glow of candlelight wrapped like a cozy blanket around her. She found the designated row of pews easily and slowly moved toward it, noticing the young, black man who sat sideways in one of the pews two rows behind it, his eyes on the entrance.

As soon as he saw her, he got to his feet and shuffled into the aisle ahead of her, brushing past her as she got closer. The young male's head tilted ever so slightly into a nod, silently acknowledging their secret connection. Once he left, she paused next to the row of seats, casting a watchful eye throughout the church. Relieved that it was entirely empty, she slipped into her allotted seat. The silence was welcoming and she drank in the holy atmosphere, basking in the safety it brought her. She could flop over onto the bench and stay there all night, she thought, as exhaustion suddenly caught up with her.

But sleeping wasn't an option right now. Time waited for no one and she was nowhere close to locating the painting—not to mention stealing it.

Once more she looked over her shoulder, making sure it was safe before her hand reached beneath her pew, patting the space underneath her seat. Her fingers found the envelope quickly and she pulled it away from the wood, then reached inside to remove its contents. Her lips curled into a smile when she found a printout of a nearby hotel reservation along with a note. She recognized Andre's handwriting that read, 'Sleep is the key to winning the battle'. She instantly knew what his words meant, grateful that he had, once again, gone the extra mile for her.

The hotel was around the corner, one of the more exclusive ones that offered a view across the river. He'd always chosen the best hotels when she was on a job somewhere, claiming she'd be more productive in a pleasant environment.

She slipped the envelope inside her jacket, securing it next to the piece of paper with the cellmate's address on. She snuck a quick glance at the scribbled information before she buried it back inside her pocket. As she took a few more moments pondering on what lay ahead, a new plan slowly took shape in her head. Perhaps there was a way to get the information she needed from Gustav's cellmate without having to use violence. Perhaps she could bribe him with money instead. And, judging from his address, she suspected money would have him singing like a canary in no time.

FROM THE DARK shadows behind the thick columns in the back of the church, Pascale watched in silence. He had seen something in the woman's eyes, something that caught his attention, made him sense there was something different about her. Perhaps it was curiosity over why she needed to get to the church so badly, or perhaps his instincts were trying to tell him something. He'd been in this business long enough to recognize the signs.

And then there was the young man who left moments after she had walked in. He had only caught a glimpse but he had seen the look in his eyes, as if he'd recognized her, as if he'd been waiting for her. Why? Who was he?

When the woman looked over her shoulder, she nearly caught sight of him, and Pascale quickly ducked behind the column, careful not to make a sound. When he was sure she hadn't seen him, he slowly stepped out again. Once more, his eyes found her and he saw her hunched over, her arm searching for something on the floor. In the hollow echoes of the church, he could hear the rustling of paper and leaned out a bit more, trying to get a better look. But it was impossible without compromising his position.

From where he stood, hidden from her, he could only see the back of her head, tipped forward as if she was praying. Guilt set in and he suddenly wondered if he'd seen something that wasn't there. Might it simply be a widow, grieving the loss of her spouse or her child? Perhaps his meeting with Gerard had his head in a tizzy, blinded by desperation, tainted by the conversations over the painting. It wouldn't be the first time his emotions clouded his judgement, and it was entirely possible that he'd found this poor woman suspicious only because his mind was already focused on finding the mystery woman they had encountered in Züber's house.

Concluding that it was all just a big misunderstanding on his part, he snuck toward the exit, determined not to fall into the trap of suspecting every beautiful woman he crossed paths with again.

AS JORJA SOAKED up the last bit of holy sustenance she desperately needed, the door to the church echoed loudly into the quiet space around her. She turned to see who had come into the church but saw no one. It made her nervous and she was suddenly reminded of the dangerous game she was a part of. Wasting no time, she jumped up and set off toward the exit. Andre had taken care of everything. He was right. She needed to rest, plan ahead. Fear had her paranoid and not thinking clearly. She had time.

She'd find a way. She would get to the bank in the morning, and once Gustav's cellmate told her where the painting was, she'd do whatever she needed to do to steal it...and get Ben back.

OUTSIDE, the streets were quiet and she hurried to the hotel, suddenly more vigilant of being followed than before. She was exhausted, but letting her guard down now could cost her everything. Satisfied she wasn't followed, she entered the hotel and made her way to the front desk, presenting the reservation number to the friendly girl who instantly greeted her with a red-lipped smile.

"Ah, yes, mademoiselle, we've been expecting you. Your luggage is already in your room. I will have the kitchen prepare your evening meal right away and send it up as soon as possible. Is there anything else you require tonight?"

"No thanks. I'm sure everything is fine." She thanked the desk clerk and followed the concierge to the elevator.

"Thanks, I'll take it from here," she told the concierge when he tried stepping into the elevator.

"Of course, mademoiselle."

Preparation was vital and, though she knew Andre's meticulous planning would have made sure her room had a proper exit strategy in place, she wanted to make sure she was prepared for every eventuality. So, when the elevator delivered her to the top floor, she found the service elevator a short walk away from her room along with the stairs to the rooftop. Two additional exits, over and above the normal stairwell, brought her instant peace, and she made her way back to her room.

As informed, her luggage was already in the room. The single luxury titanium suitcase stood at the foot of her bed and she quickly moved to open it. The combination was the same number they'd always used and her fingers glided over the numbered dials before it sprung open. Scooping the items of clothing Andre had bought for her onto the bed, her attention quickly moved to the base, where she tapped the keycard against one of the corners. As expected, the mechanism clicked open and she relished in the memory it brought. The clever idea was Ben's, which he had invented during one of their more complicated robberies. He had designed the tech to synchronize with the hotel's door key the moment they wheeled the luggage past the door. The process took less than a second and they had used it many times in the past to sneak illegal items past security.

The hidden compartment in the base of the suitcase lifted easily and she picked up the items that were buried beneath the false bottom.

A new passport bearing the same identity she always used whenever she was in Geneva, a small pearl-handle revolver along with its dual use thigh or ankle holster, a pair of black gloves, a set of lock picks, sunglasses, and a digital code-grabbing device.

Andre had considered everything, she thought, as she stared at the items on the foot of her bed. But, as she transferred the items back into the hidden compartment, she couldn't stop the doubt that settled in the back of her mind. It had been so long since she used any of these tools, since she had to steal a painting. What if she'd forgotten how to do it? What if, this time, she was reckless and got caught? What if she couldn't deliver Ben's ransom and Sokolov killed him?

She shut the case, hoping to shut her mind to the questions that now tormented her weary soul along with it. In the window opposite her, she caught her reflection, barely recognizing the timid-looking woman it belonged to. Behind her image, the city lights lined the banks of the glistening river that snaked past the hotel. Like the mighty waters of the Red Sea, she'd need to cross it to survive, to save Ben, to save herself. And just like Moses, she'd have to place her trust in God, even if she hadn't fully come to know His power yet.

She looked away from the river, up into the night sky, and spotted a dark cloud. Its edges were lined with the silvery glow of the full moon's light that lay hidden behind it. Taking it as a sign that God was indeed in control, she dropped back onto the bed, her eyes fixed on its beauty as she drifted off into a peaceful night's sleep.

CHAPTER ELEVEN

Jorja settled into the blue-and-red striped seat onboard the train. She plopped her pastry and take-away coffee atop the small table in front of her. Glancing at her wristwatch, she knew from having scanned the electronic timetable earlier that the train wouldn't leave for another seven minutes, and she rested her head back against the headrest.

She had woken up early after she had the best sleep she'd had in a long while, showered, then headed to the bank. Withdrawing her money had gone down without a hitch, making it easy to leave some behind at the hotel while she'd kept enough aside with which to bribe the cell-mate into telling her where the painting was.

Conscious of the cash she had stuffed inside the pockets of her jacket, she straightened the bulges it made around her midriff and pulled the zip higher toward her neck.

As she waited for the train to leave the station, she picked at her pastry, studying the passengers who rushed onto the train. It wouldn't hurt to remain vigilant.

The line was a popular one, with the route ending in Bern just short of two hours later. Once at her destination, she'd grab a taxi to drop her a block away from where she'd need to be, and, if all went well and the ex-con took her bribe, she should be back at her hotel by mid afternoon to strategize the heist.

Hope filled her and the prospect of it all working out and getting Ben back safely brought a slight smile to her lips. She *could* do this. She wasn't too old and she hadn't forgotten her skills. She could finally put it to use for the greater good and put her past behind her, start over with Ben and with God.

HER PLAN HAD SO FAR GONE DOWN smoothly, and Jorja soon found herself a block away from the address she strong-armed out of Gustav's parole officer. The taxi driver had reluctantly dropped her off as she asked, but he had urged her to reconsider her request. According to him the area was one of the rougher suburbs of Switzerland's capital city, known to be one where gangs frequented and trouble was never far away. But, regardless of the risks the driver proceeded to warn her of, Jorja had insisted that she would be fine and stepped out onto the white concrete sidewalk. Although she had every intention not to use it, she had fastened the small revolver to her ankle, concealing it beneath her denim jeans while she left the larger gun in her luggage at the hotel. Upon first glance, the suburb didn't look half as bad as the taxi driver had described it, but once she turned the corner and walked down the next street, she suddenly felt as if a million eyes were upon her.

And her instincts weren't far off when she was soon confronted by three men who blocked her way. Not wanting any trouble, she attempted to cross to the other side of the road, only to have them do the same. Two more thugs joined the men, and, like wolves descending on a carcass, more poured from the houses out onto the sidewalks around her. Determined not to show the fear that made her limbs tremble, she pushed her hands deeper inside her pockets to where they pressed up against the wads of cash that were concealed inside her jacket. Surrounded by gangsters, she stopped in the middle of the road, suddenly regretting the decision to leave her higher capacity gun at the hotel.

FROM THE ROW of dilapidated housing, a few lowlifes stood outside on their porches and steps, snickering back and forth as they watched the display of intimidation play off in the street. Whistles of flirtation echoed into the air, tempting her to start running in fear, but she stood firm, carefully assessing each of her threats. One of the men lunged forward then receded again between his peers in a mocking attempt to scare her. But, in spite of the fact that her heart threatened to explode in her chest, her body remained still and unshaken. The lack of reaction toward his intimidation taunts had the man instantly flush with embarrassment before his eyes fearfully trailed to a man who stood leaning against a post on his porch. His face and exposed parts of his neck and hands were entirely covered in tattoos, the sheer volume of it making it seem as if he had a green-tinged second skin beneath his clothing. Of average build, he didn't look threatening, but it was very evident from the watchful glances he got that he was indeed the ringleader of the pack.

Having established the source of the gang's power, Jorja resorted to intimidation tactics of her own and turned her sights toward him instead. The slight flicker in his eyes and change of stance told her that he hadn't intended on being figured out, giving her the confirmation of his authoritarian position that she was looking for. She held her silent gaze, squared her shoulders, and waited.

The crowd of subordinates grew louder, desperate to deflect the attention away from their leader. But Jorja ignored them and turned to face their leader head on. As if pledging their allegiance to him by putting on a show, the three men slowly moved in on her.

Still, Jorja held her position, because showing fear and

vulnerability were what men like these preyed upon and she refused to be intimidated in giving them what they wanted. Instead, in the quiet corners of her soul, she asked God to protect her, to help her, to settle the fear that weighed so heavily in her heart.

When the men were upon her, the largest of the three attempted to stroke the back of her head. Without warning, Jorja's arm twisted around his forearm, immobilizing him by simultaneously forcing his fingers back until he squealed in pain. With his head now facing her feet, she, thrust her knee into his jaw, leaving behind a large cut on his mouth. She pushed him back against his posse, who didn't hesitate to take a few steps back. One raised his small fists in front of his face, the other revealed his switchblade. Undeterred by the threatening position the thugs held over her, Jorja stood her ground, her eyes fixed on the ringleader instead. A slight nod from him told his men to go at her again. They did. First the larger one whose arm she nearly broke, then the guy carrying the knife. It would take a calculated forceful move, but he was the easiest to fight off and, while ducking the large one's oncoming fist, she scissor-kicked the blade from his hands, then followed with a quick shoe in his face that left his nose broken and bleeding. As soon as the larger one came at her again, she once more avoided his fist before the base of her palm smashed below the goatee on his chin. His head thrust back and she finished him off by driving a flat hand, pinkie side first, into his Adam's apple. Gasping for air and gagging, he stumbled back, shoving the smallest of the three thugs out of the way in the process.

When the trio surrendered by crawling into hiding, Jorja once again turned her gaze to the gang leader, who'd been watching his men get whipped in less than thirty seconds.

Fully aware that he hadn't given any of his other subordinates the go-ahead to attack her, Jorja tipped her head forward in the slightest of nods before she pushed past the defeated opponents and proceeded to walk along the street. Behind her, laughter at the three losers broke out and she instantly knew she had won the battle. She held her steady gait, forcing herself not to look back. She had done the impossible. They had backed away, even though she knew they could have easily drawn on their numbers and killed her. When she was a fair distance away and out of their crosshairs, she stopped for the first time, realizing her victory was nothing short of a David and Goliath moment, and that through divine intervention, God had stepped in and she had escaped unharmed. She thanked God for his protection, drew on the confidence it gave her, and vowed to never doubt Him again.

WHEN SHE NEARED THE HOUSE, she paused on the sidewalk. She had spotted the front door that stood ajar. The house looked like it was in dire need of repairs. It was missing a few roof tiles, some floorboards on the steps and porch were broken, and almost all of the gray paint on the timber walls was stripped away. She looked up and down the street. Apart from the silver blue sedan that stood opposite the neighbor's house, there were only a few cars parked further down the road. The street was completely quiet.

Behind her, a dreary-looking German Shepherd suddenly barked and she looked back to find it wrestling against the chain that fastened him to a hook in the ground, his focus aimed at something to her left. She ignored it and turned her attention back to the house that remained undisturbed as a feeling of unrest came over her. Her hand found the piece of paper with the address on in her pocket and she quickly checked that she had the correct address. She did, so she proceeded to walk up the short garden path and onto the small porch.

To her left, a noise sounded from the narrow gateway on the side of the house, and she stopped to listen. She could hear movement and faint whispers. She held back from going onto the small porch towards the front door and waited, heard the gate swing open.

Then, she saw them.

CHAPTER TWELVE

Two men ran alongside the house, past the edge of the porch where they stopped and crouched down. They were an odd pair. One tall and athletic with pitch black hair, while the other was the exact opposite with flaxen hair, much shorter in height, and beefy in build. At first they didn't see her, but then one spotted her. He looked up, his sunflower blond hair blowing away from his face in the light breeze to expose his bushy, fair eyebrows and startled eyes. For the briefest of seconds he locked eyes with Jorja, and she saw something familiar in them. His demeanor told her there was more to the encounter than the obvious surprise that came with her presence when he quickly hid behind his partner's tall frame. Their voices raised, an anxious exchange of words between them had them darting down the short driveway and into the silver blue car that was parked opposite the street. As they sped off, Jorja searched for the vehicle's license plate but found that it didn't have one. Now, more convinced than ever, Jorja knew something was amiss. At first she thought of running, for fear of what she might find inside, but then she knew she couldn't turn away empty handed. This was her only lead to finding the painting and she had to chance it.

Careful not to touch the doorknob, she pushed the wood with the nose of her shoe until the gap was big enough for her to slip through. The door creaked on its hinges but, once inside, the house was eerily silent.

She allowed herself to take in the cramped space around her. Unable to move two feet without stepping on something, it was clear that there had been a struggle, or that the men were looking for something. Could it be that she merely stumbled upon a burglary, or were they there for the same reason she was?

Moving around the single brown velour sofa that stood sideways and out of place in the room, she walked throughout the small house in search of the man she'd come there to see. The kitchen was a mess and the putrid smell that permeated from it briefly had her catch her breath as she passed through it. Dirty dishes covered every surface space while the fridge stood ajar exposing nothing but a dozen or so beers and a pizza box. Strewn throughout the floor, all the drawers and their contents lay on the black-and-white tiled floor. They were definitely searching for something, she concluded.

She moved down the small, dark passage, but there was still no sign of anyone else inside the house. But when she stepped over the threshold of the master bedroom at the end of the hallway, all that changed in an instant.

The mutilated body of a man, whom she could only assume was the one she'd come there to see, lay across the bed. A sight of torture so ghastly that she had to make a run for the bathroom to rid herself of the sick that could not be held down. When she was done, she flushed the loo and wiped her fingerprints from the handle before she made her way back to the sitting room. In the far distance she heard police sirens and listened to hear if they were drawing closer.

They were, and she wasted no time to make a hasty departure. When her feet hit the sidewalk she dashed across the street, briefly glancing at the dog whose incessant barking stung her ears as she passed him. She picked up her pace, conscious of the sirens that grew louder with each passing second. Despair overwhelmed her and nearly made her legs collapse beneath her body. Her only chance of finding the painting and freeing Ben had seeped into the bloodied sheets beneath the cellmate's dead body. And there was now no way of remedying the situation.

OUT IN FRONT of her the street stretched into the distance. With houses on either side, there was nowhere to hide. Along with her hopes and plans to get out from the mess she'd made of her life, she was downright trapped.

Behind her, the police cars screeched to a halt in front of the house. She was only three doors down. If she ran now it would draw suspicion to her. All she could do was blend in with the curious residents who now rushed out into their gardens and onto the street. Deciding it was her only option, she joined a small group of women who had come out of the nearby house and stood in awe speculating over the happenings. They were speaking German, not French, and she had no understanding as to what they were saying. She heard one mention the cellmate's name and Jorja listened more intently, desperate to comprehend the conversation that ensued. Soon after, the same woman made a call from her bright pink bedazzled mobile phone. When she spoke into the phone she switched to speaking French and Jorja felt the tension instantly leave her stomach in relief that she could now understand what was being discussed.

The young woman caller's voice turned gentle as she cautiously told the person on the other end of the phone about the police, then proceeded to tell the recipient to come home. A panicked female voice echoed through the device and Jorja listened as the woman consoled her. When she had ended the call, Jorja took the opportunity to ask the caller if she knew what was going on. Jorja's French was fluent so none of the women were any wiser that she was an outsider.

"What's with all the police?" Jorja asked, sounding as relaxed as she could considering what she had already seen.

"Not sure, but it must be bad for them to send so many cars. The cops don't usually bother much with us. We're apparently more hassle to them than anything else."

The girl's answer was tainted with scorn, as if this type of action was a regular occurrence in the neighborhood.

"Whose house is it, do you know?"

"Of course, everyone knows it's Jürgen's house. You from out of town?"

"Yes, I was just passing through," Jorja quickly said, grateful that her answer seemed to have settled any suspicion.

"We've been telling Ana for months now to stay away from the guy. He's been nothing but trouble since he got out of jail. But she's so in love with the deadbeat that she can't see clearly. Isn't it the truth, girls?" She invited the other girls' input who collectively agreed without hesitation.

"Are they married?" Jorja asked again.

The girl sucked the air inside her cheek in scoffing. "The stupid girl got engaged to him two weeks ago. I told her it was a mistake, but she's not listening. They've been at it for years, sending letters back and forth when he was still locked up. He did a real number on her if you ask me."

They watched as the police started taping off the area in front of the house. A short while later, a pretty girl in her early twenties pulled into the road in a bright yellow Fiat Punto and rushed toward the guarding police officers. Frantic screams erupted as the police told her she shouldn't go in and that her fiancé was found dead in the house.

"I'll go get her," one of the women next to Jorja shouted back as she already set off toward her.

"Poor thing," Jorja seized the moment in a desperate effort to learn more about her. If Ana was indeed Jürgen's fiancé, and they'd been writing to each other while he was still in prison, there was a good chance he might have shared details about the painting with her. It was worth a shot, she thought.

But neither of the three women who stood watching their friend cross the street toward them gave her any sort of reply. Their focus wasn't on frivolous talk anymore. Under the protective embrace of her friend, Jorja watched as Ana walked toward them, tears streaming down her heavily makeup-ed face. As she drew closer and Jorja was able to have a better look at her, it was evident from her attire that she was quite possibly an exotic dancer. Her silver platform stiletto sandals elongated her slim black fishnet-clad legs to where they disappeared under an over-sized navy-and-red striped sweater she must have pulled on in her haste to get there. When she allowed the small huddle to welcome her in, her slouchy gold handbag slipped off her arm and fell in a shimmering pile to the ground beneath their feet. Her compassionate circle of friends ushered her toward the house behind them and Jorja scooped the bag from the curb, grateful for the unforeseen opportunity it now presented. As a glimmer of newfound hope flickered on the horizon, Jorja quietly trailed behind as she followed them into the house.

CHAPTER THIRTEEN

The silver blue sedan raced past the police cars, its drivers grateful that they had managed to escape their pursuit in time. The stocky blond was already dialing the short number on his mobile when they turned the next corner and drove toward their getaway.

The man on the other end answered with a short 'yes?' and the blond didn't hesitate to jump straight into his report.

"She saw us! She was there," he said, as he looked back over his shoulder as if someone was chasing after them.

"Who?" the man on the other end of the line said calmly.

"The woman, from Züber's place. She caught us leaving the house."

"Did you get what you were supposed to?"

"What? No, the guy was already dead. It's not like we

can get information from a corpse. And to make things worse, now she's seen our faces, and I'm a hundred percent sure she recognized me. I could see it in her eyes."

"And?"

"And? The police are already there. We almost got caught. If she tells them about us, they'll come after us and we go down for a murder we didn't commit! This wasn't the plan. I'm not going down for someone else's crime. You said—"

"But you didn't kill the guy so there's nothing to worry about, right?"

The blond was suddenly at a loss for words.

"Sure, but that doesn't change the fact that she was there. I've been doing this a long time and it was no coincidence that she was there. What aren't you telling us? If you're hiding something, we have a right to know." The beefy man squared his shoulders as he looked to his friend for support. From behind the wheel the friend nodded in agreement, encouraging his fair-haired friend to stand his ground against their employer.

"Let's not forget who's paying you to do this job. I want you to do what you were instructed to do in the first place. Find out what the guy knew and where that painting is, and don't come back until you find me something to work with. Understood?"

The phone clicked off in the blond guy's ear and he threw it against the dashboard, dropping a few curses as he did so. He reached for a cigarette and dragged back hard to expose a bright glowing ring around the tip where the paper burned away. When he relaxed a bit, his tall friend spoke.

"What now?"

The blond swore again. "He wants us to go back and find out what the dead guy knew. Can you believe it? How are we supposed to go in there now with the place swarming with cops? He's lost his mind. What's so special about this painting anyway? They have too much money on their hands, that's what it is."

"And what about the woman? Did he say anything?"

"Nothing, he's not even bothered by her. But I tell you, she recognized me, I'm sure of it. She's the same one."

"So what? She knows nothing."

"Maybe, but he knows more than he is telling us. I can smell a rat a mile off, and he's a fat one."

"The fact is they pay our bills, and handsomely, I might add. Let's hang low until the cops leave and then we go back. Maybe we missed something in the rush. With the house quiet and off limits we might have a better chance of finding something."

The blond agreed that his partner made sense and they set off to the nearest bar to drown their sorrows until it was safe for them to return to the house.

PASCALE LUPIN'S thumbs rapped anxiously on the black leather of his car's steering wheel. His eyes darted cautiously between the rear view mirrors and the road ahead as he firmed his grip around the wheel and shuffled restlessly in his seat.

His car pushed along the lonely road that snaked between tall trees toward the remote location he visited the same time every week. Usually, he'd be a lot more relaxed, but this week's meeting had him on edge.

It's the closest he'd been to the end of his mission in years, yet, once again, the trail ran dead, literally. Just thinking about it again as he pushed the car faster up a slight slope, made his blood boil. He'd come so close this time, but once again Gerard Dubois was one step ahead of him. He was too influential and too experienced. Feeling defeated once more, he was convinced the man couldn't be beaten.

And, just as he had nearly done a dozen times before over the past seven years, Pascale was ready to walk away. He had had enough. Today was the day he'd finally bow out gracefully, call it quits, surrender defeat. Perhaps he'd been too close to it all these years. Perhaps it was time he stepped away and left Gerard Dubois to be someone else's problem.

It would be easy enough to disappear, he thought. He had money and he had the means to get a new identity. At fifty-two he had spent nearly half his life pretending to be someone he wasn't anyway, except, this time it would be for his benefit alone. Heaven knows he hadn't had a vacation in nearly ten years.

When he noticed the time on the dashboard, he dropped a gear and sped the car faster along the road. If there was one particular day he didn't want to be late, it would be today. He had rehearsed his speech a dozen times in the mirror that morning. It would be short and sweet, with the result that would, for once, leave him feeling in control of his own life once again.

With newfound courage to do what needed to be done, he took the final turn toward the remote truck stop. It had served him well over the years. But, seeing it draw closer up ahead suddenly made him second-guess his decision to quit his mission.

"Darn it! Stupid determination!" he shouted as his hand slammed against the steering wheel.

For he knew Pascale Lupin was no quitter. It simply wasn't in his make-up. It's what made him the best, what *had* made him the best for nearly three decades. He couldn't throw in the towel even if he wanted to. He had worked too hard, given up too much, sacrificed his entire life. Giving Gerard Dubois what he deserved had been what he lived and breathed for. It was his addiction, his drug of choice. He couldn't let him win. He couldn't stop, not now.

When his car turned off the road and drove into the truck stop that was mostly concealed from the road behind a row of tall, dense trees and shrubs, the black SUV was already waiting for him.

He parked his car behind it and took the few strides he needed to get into the rear seat. His boss greeted him with a friendly pat on the back as he settled into the plush leather seat next to him.

"How are you, my boy? Are you holding up?" the much older man enquired gently.

Pascale merely nodded, still in agony over whether to proceed or quit.

"You look troubled. What's up?"

"We hit a dead end. Again. The guy is smart, I'll give him that," Pascal reported.

"And you want to give up."

Pascale's eyes met his other employer's. He had been like a father to him and he knew him well, too well.

"I can't do this anymore. I'll never outsmart Dubois. The guy is always ten steps ahead of me. How he does it, I yet have to discover, but I can't live like this anymore. My entire life is a farce. Heck, I don't even know who I am anymore. I don't want to turn into someone I'm not. It's not worth it anymore."

When he had blurted out his jumbled speech, he waited for his boss and longtime mentor to respond, but he didn't. He merely sat there, hands folded in his lap, staring into Pascale's eyes.

"Aren't you going to say something?" Pascale eventually broke the awkward silence.

"Like what?"

"Anything. Say something." His voice sounded desperate and childish.

"If you want me to tell you that I'm okay with what you're saying and that I give you permission to quit, that's not going to happen. I've never known you to quit anything, ever. You're a fighter, always have been. That's what makes you so good at your job."

Pascale rubbed his palms over his eyes then up and down his thighs. Inside, his emotions were raging out of control. Part of him wanted to run. As far away from everyone and everything as his feet would allow. But the other part needed to stay, wanted to stay, to see this through to the end.

"Why don't you just tell me what's tripped you up, son, then we can find a way past it?"

"That's just it, I don't know if there is a way through this. I'm in too deep, it's a mess and I can't see how I'm going to turn this around."

"Let's try anyway. Humor me."

Pascale took a deep breath and proceeded to report every detail of his past week. About Züber's death, the life-line that led to his ex-cellmate which ran dead with a murder he was certain was ordered by Gerard Dubois, and the mysterious woman who seems to have suddenly popped up out of nowhere and who was somehow entangled in it all. And when he had gotten it all out and on the table, it was the simple words of his mentor that instantly melted the wall of ice that had blocked him from seeing a way through.

"Find a way to make the woman your friend instead of your enemy. Do that and you'll be back in the game. She knows something we don't. Forget about Dubois for now, and set your focus on her. We have resources, Pascale. Use them."

CHAPTER FOURTEEN

When Ana's tears finally dried up and the girls stopped smothering her with sympathy, she looked up at Jorja with questions in her eyes.

"Who's she? I haven't moved out yet! I'm still paying rent here, you know." Her voice blasted accusations toward her girlfriends.

"Hey, babes, chill. She's not moving in. She's just someone who passed by. Actually, who are you?" One's attention turned to Jorja.

"No one important. Sorry, I didn't mean to impose." Jorja handed Ana her handbag.

"Then why are you here?"

Jorja felt her throat close up as her mind searched for something to say. She had to find out if Ana knew anything about the painting. She was her last hope.

"I knew your fiancé's cellmate. He's dead too. I came

here hoping to speak to Jürgen about something but now he's...sorry."

Ana jumped to her feet, her eyes suddenly blazing with heat, her chest heaving forward in attack.

"You're one of them, aren't you? Did you kill him? Why, huh, what could you possibly have wanted with him?"

Two girls held her small frame back and tried calming her down, but their eyes were suddenly alive with accusation too.

"No, never! I didn't kill anyone. And I'm on my own. I came here to speak to him. He was already dead when I got there, I swear!" Jorja defended.

"About what? What could someone like you possibly want to speak to my Jürgen about? You're not exactly his type." Ana's eyes filled with fresh tears.

"It's not like that at all. Like I said, I knew the man he'd shared a prison cell with and I just needed to ask him a few things, that's all."

Ana slumped back onto the sofa and started digging around in her handbag on her lap. When she found her pack of cigarettes, she lit one and sat back in the sofa, one arm crossed around her thin waist while the other held her cigarette.

"It's about that stupid painting, isn't it?"

Her question threw Jorja off guard, surprise blatantly visible on her face.

"I thought so. That's precisely why he's now dead. I told him to let it go, warned him it would be the death of him, but did he listen? No! He was so stupid." Ana buried her face in the oversized fabric around her wrist, the cigarette glowing in front of her forehead.

"You know about the painting?"

"Of course I know about the painting. Jürgs and I didn't have secrets. He told me everything."

Jorja sat on the low coffee table that stood opposite Ana and forced her eyes on hers.

"Ana, I know you've been through a lot, and I know you loved Jürgen and won't do anything to taint his memory, but it's important you tell me everything you know about that painting."

Ana scoffed. "You're joking, right? Why would I do that, huh? Clearly it's what got him killed. The less I have to do with it the better. I might not be as classy as you, but I know a thing or two about people like you. You use people like Jürgs and me to get what you want, even if it means you kill for it. I'm not telling you anything so just leave!"

"I agree, you should leave," one of the other girls echoed.

"No, wait, listen, it's not like that. I'm not here to use you and I had nothing to do with your fiancé's death. I'm trying to do the right thing here, that's all. I need that painting, please. Just tell me what you know."

But Ana remained silent as her friends moved to physically pull Jorja away from her and get her out of their home.

"Ana, I don't know who killed Jürgen, but I do know

they're dangerous. They have friends, as dangerous if not more. And those friends nearly killed me too. If I don't bring them that painting they're going to kill the only true friend I've ever had. Please, you have to help me!"

Perhaps it was something in Jorja's desperate plea, or perhaps it was the tears that now rolled uncontrollably down her cheeks that had Ana and her friends suddenly pause to reassess their opinions, but the room fell silent around them.

It was Ana who finally spoke first.

"I don't understand. I know it's worth a lot, but why this one? What's so important about this stupid painting that people have to die over it?"

Her question was the glimmer of hope Jorja had been seeking and she didn't hesitate to tell them.

"Have you ever heard of a famous painter named Leonardo Da Vinci?"

The girls shook their heads in near unison.

"How about the *Mona Lisa*?"

"Yes, of course we all know that one," one of the girls answered quickly.

"Well, Da Vinci was the guy who painted the *Mona Lisa*, but he also painted the *Salvator Mundi*, an exquisite oil canvas of Christ the Savior."

"You mean, Jesus," Ana said.

"Yes, however, unlike the *Mona Lisa*, this painting has been missing for years. No one has ever been able to find it after it went missing following an auction. It never made it to its destination."

"Yeah, I know all this already. So what?"

"You know this, how?" Jorja asked, intrigued.

"Jürgs told me, of course. I told you, we didn't have any secrets between us."

"What else did he tell you, Ana?"

"Oh, no, see, there you go again, thinking you can dupe me into telling you stuff. I'm not going to betray Jürgen, even if he's dead."

"Ana, I'm not asking you to betray him. He'd already told my friend, his cellmate. That's how I knew to come speak with him. They were planning to get it back."

"I know, that's what would've gotten us out of this rubbish hole we've been stuck living in. We had it all planned out. We were going to leave Europe and find our own piece of paradise. Somewhere far away from everyone and everything that had it in for us. Now he's dead and I'm still stuck in that nightclub working for his loser boss. I'm never going to get out now."

Fresh tears soaked her sleeves as her friends, once again, consoled her.

"You should go, really. We're sorry for your friend, but Ana's been through enough," one of the girls next to her said.

But Jorja knew if she had any chance of getting Sokolov what he wanted, she'd have to persuade Ana to talk. So, she shrugged off the friends' grip and leaned in closer to Ana's face.

"Look, Ana, I can't stop your heart from hurting, and I can't bring Jürgen back, but I can help you get away and still live the life you had planned to have with him."

When she saw that she'd caught Ana's attention, Jorja continued. "I know what it means to run and hide from your past. I've done it for twenty years, successfully, and I can help you do it too. I have a friend who is able to create a new identity for you, give you a passport and everything. And I can give you money, enough to get you to your paradise and set you up for at least a year until you find a better way of earning an honest living. I'll make it happen for you if you tell me everything Jürgen told you."

Ana looked at her friends for input, and when she'd found in their eyes what her heart had already decided, she wiped her eyes with her sleeves and said, "Can you really do everything you just said you can, for me?"

Jorja smiled, her heart overjoyed that she had managed to earn victory over the situation.

"Absolutely, and I'll prove it to you right now." She took out three tight bundles of large bills and held it out for Ana to take. "I'll get the rest of the money and your new passport to you within twenty-four-hours if you help me. I don't have a lot of time left."

Ana's slim fingers curled around the cash, nearly dropping the cigarette she had pinched between two of her fingers.

"This is a lot of money."

"Yes, it is, and I'll make true on my promise to give you the rest. You can start a new life, Ana. Away from the pain, away from the life you're forced to live."

Ana's eyes hadn't left the cash that now lay in her lap. Two of her friends flanked her sides and quietly encouraged her to take the deal.

"If they find out that Jürgen told me they'll kill me too."

"Who, Ana, who?"

"My boss, Jürgen's boss. I know they killed him."

"Why do you think that?"

"Because he'd been trying to leave the *Gardiens* ever since he got out of prison."

CHAPTER FIFTEEN

Jorja waited for Ana to tell her more but the petite girl with the fiery spirit suddenly fell silent.

"It's okay, Ana, you can trust me."

"I don't even know your name. How can I trust you?"

"Jorja, Jorja Rose, and you can trust me as much as I am choosing to trust you."

"It's a nice name," Ana said, after a long pause as her lips curled into a faint smile that told Jorja it was safe to probe her more.

"Tell me about the *Gardiens*. Is the name French, meaning guardians? Are they a mob?"

Ana nodded.

"I've never heard of them."

"Why should you? You don't strike me as the kind who gets mixed up with them. They're one of, if not the biggest and most powerful, mob in all of Europe, probably the world. You don't mess with these people. As far as I know the big boss orders hits like he's ordering his caviar if you as much as think out of line. They say he lives somewhere here in Geneva but no one knows for sure. From what I hear, he has cells operating everywhere and none of them have ever seen the guy, much less met him. Jürgen was thirteen when he joined the mob and he hadn't even come close to meeting him. Most of them never do. They report to their leader and he communicates to another guy, and so on. Like Chinese whispers. Jürgs was higher up the ranks so he reported directly to Franz."

"He's your boss, at the club?"

"Yes, I only took the job to get close to him so I could spy on him. Jürgs thought that me being on the inside was the only way of getting into his safe. I was meant to keep him occupied while some guy broke into the safe."

Soft cries escaped from her throat as she spoke. "Now Jürgs is dead and I'm still stuck on the inside."

"I'm going to get you out, Ana, I promise. Tell me about the safe. What's in the safe?"

Ana took a deep breath before she answered.

"As far as I know, Franz was in charge of the cell who had stolen the painting. Jürgen was in that cell." She dropped her head in shame over the part her dead fiancé had in it, then continued. "That's why he went to prison: the police caught them, but Franz managed to escape with the painting. That's how he moved up the ranks to club owner. He finished the job and got the payout while Jürgs and the others went to jail. All he knew was that the painting was bought by some rich guy in Dubai, I think."

"Abu Dhabi."

"Yes, that's the one. They all sound the same to me," she shrugged.

Jorja's body lit up at the hint of getting the information she so desperately needed. Excitement surged through her body while she digested what she'd just heard.

"Wait, let me make sure I understand you correctly. You're saying, no, confirming, that the *Salvator Mundi* was in fact stolen during transit by a European mob known as the *Gardiens*?"

Ana nodded and Jorja was suddenly on her feet, her body alive and tingling throughout.

"I can't believe the rumors are true. The painting *was* intercepted between the auction and the buyer. All these years...," She paused, then laughed jubilantly before she once more hastily took her seat on the table across from Ana.

"And you're saying Franz has the whereabouts of the painting locked up in his safe. Where's his safe?"

"I think so, yes. Jürgs said he met a guy who knew everything there is to know about these paintings and that he'd made a deal with the guy to help us steal the painting, take back what Franz owed him. He had a buyer lined up for it and everything. But now all that's gone up in a cloud of smoke and Franz is still living the good life leeching off people like me." Ana once again broke down in tears and Jorja leaned forward to take her hands in hers.

"Ana, look at me. That guy on the inside's name was Züber and I'm the one he was going to use to steal the painting. I used to be an art thief, a good one, actually. Züber and I worked together for many years before he went to prison for art fraud." She intentionally left out her involvement in turning on him and skipped ahead to the dire situation she now found herself in. "Back then we'd gotten involved with a dangerous man—the buyer—and now he wants payback by getting the painting that was promised to him. He's blackmailing me into stealing it for him in exchange for my friend's life. That's why I'm here and with what you've just told me, I can get us both out of this for good. But I can't do it alone. I'm going to need your help. All you need to do is tell me where the safe is and I will do the rest."

Ana pinned her eyes on Jorja's face, as if she still needed convincing that it was okay to trust her. It was only once she buried the cash deep inside her bag that Jorja knew she had won her over. She waited for Ana to speak and, after what seemed like forever, she finally did.

"I can get you into the club and tell you where the safe is, but then you're on your own. If Franz as much as sniffs my involvement in this I am as good as dead."

"Deal!" Jorja exclaimed, and stretched one hand to shake on it.

Ana shook hands before she lit another cigarette.

"He's got a meeting tonight, in the private lounge. Some guy who comes there every week to see him. I think he's one of them. Franz usually has Lucy assigned to serve their table—he has a thing for her, but I know her kid is sick so I'll offer to help her out. That way I can keep an eye out for you. Their meetings are never longer than about an hour, sometimes less, so you'll have to be quick."

"That's more than I'll need. Tell me about the safe."

"It's hidden behind a secret panel in the wall of his office. I'm not sure how he opens the panel but he's usually next to his desk when it happens."

"Got it, and what about the safe, what does it look like?"

"Not like the ones you get with the buttons. Jürgs said it couldn't be opened without the combination code because it's got the round knob that you turn."

"Perfect, it's a permutation lock. I'll be in and out in less than ten minutes."

Ana raised an eyebrow in response.

"Really? You're that good?"

"I am." She smiled then continued. "Now, what time is the meeting?"

WITH HIS MENTOR'S words still humming in his head, Pascale decided to walk to the club instead of having his driver drop him off as he usually did when he checked in on Gerard's affairs. It was a beautiful evening and he needed the fresh air and time to gather his thoughts. Once again, he had allowed his employer to persuade him not to give up. And though his heart agreed, his mind was still not convinced. He was tired of living a double life, tired of the danger it brought, and the risks that were increasing faster than he had time to prepare.

Watching his back, had become an exhausting task and, even with the security his relationship with Gabrielle provided, he hadn't slept properly in years. But he had worked too hard to throw in the towel now and he was close, very close. So close he could almost touch it.

As he neared the club, he shifted his focus onto business instead. At least the meetings with Franz were normally easygoing and, as always, wouldn't take much of his time. Franz was sleazy and he hated going into his club, but the man's allegiance to the *Gardiens* was faultless and he ran his books with great integrity and accuracy. His club served as one of their biggest laundry pits and if there was one thing Gerard valued more than anything, it was loyalty.

Pausing on the sidewalk in front of the club, he glanced at his watch. He could be done and dusted by nine, which would leave him ample time to go past the church on his way home. With any luck, the woman might be there again and that's all he needed: an opportunity. And once he got one, he'll follow his mentor's council and find a way of getting close to her. He was right. He could use her to get what he wanted. If he could find out who she was and what she was after, he could find a way to end this.

CHAPTER SIXTEEN

When Pascale stepped inside the dark club, the brawny doormen received him with a friendly welcome before a petite hostess took over and led him toward the small glass-domed private lounge.

"Franz will be with you in a sec," she said as she seated him.

"Where's Lucy?" Pascale asked when the usual hostess was nowhere to be seen. Conversations like theirs were best kept confidential and he'd come to trust Lucy's presence during their meetings over the years.

"Her kid's sick so she's off tonight. But don't worry, I'll take good care of you this evening. You won't even know she's not here. I'm Ana, by the way." She smiled as she turned toward the glass door. "I'll go get your drink to loosen you up while I find out what's keeping Franz." She flashed him another smile and quickly disappeared behind the glass door.

Pascale watched as the girl moved between the tables toward the bar. It didn't hurt to keep an eye on her, just in case. It was part of his job to make sure their meetings weren't breached and he already knew she hadn't been working there for long. And, although he trusted Franz to have run all the usual security checks on her, it would be remiss of him to drop his guard. His eyes trailed her as she bounced between two customer tables, finishing off their orders before she returned to the bar to collect his drink. As she made her way back, he eyeballed Franz stepping out from behind the dark purple velvet drapes in the back of the club. His face showed signs of worry as he walked up to Ana from behind and said, what Pascale could only read to have been, a stern reminder of what he was expecting from her during his meeting. The girl's face mirrored Pascale's suspicions and he instantly spotted the nerves that had her body suddenly tense up as they entered the glass enclosure.

"Sorry I'm late, Pascale. Sometimes I feel like firing everyone." He took his seat at the table and looked at Ana who hovered to his right. "Must I spell it out or are you going to bring me my drink?"

His words were sharp and had Ana instantly spin around and head to the bar.

"Stupid woman. Can't live with them, can't live without them, huh?" He winked sleazily at Pascale then slouched back in his chair before he continued his degrading rant at the female species.

Pascale let him go on for a bit, using the small opportunity to keep a watchful eye on Ana. He had seen something in the way she looked at Franz. Something he couldn't quite put his finger on yet, but it had sent signs of warning into his gut. As if she knew something Franz didn't. And when Ana looked over her shoulder one too many times, briefly slowing down to say something in passing to the lonely customer who was seated at a table stationed directly next to the purple doorway that led to Franz's office, his suspicions were confirmed. His muscles in his shoulders tensed as he now turned his attention to the customer. A young male with a baseball cap and a black leather jacket. The man kept his head down as he quickly got up the moment Ana reached the bar where she flirted with the barman as if to distract him. Pascale watched as the young male quietly disappeared behind the purple curtain. Dread dropped in his stomach as his eyes remained pinned on the velvet curtain that slipped into place behind him.

"Hey, Pascale, did you not hear a word I said?" Franz called his attention back to the meeting.

"Sorry, I...how well do you know Ana?" Pascal asked.

His question stunned Franz.

"Ana? You mean the stupid girl who can't seem to hurry up with my drink?" He turned back to find her still flirting with the barman.

"Yes, her, how long has she been here?"

"Oh, not long, but I wouldn't worry about her. She's harmless. She's Jürgen's fiancé. He vouched for her."

"You don't know. Jürgen is dead."

Franz sat up in his chair.

"Dead? How?"

"The order came from upstairs. Seems he'd been blabbering off his mouth on the inside. It was necessary to protect the *Gardiens*."

"And you think he might have blabbered to Ana too." He let out a few curse words.

"I don't know, but I would watch my back if I were you."

Their conversation was interrupted when Ana re-entered with Franz's drink.

"Took you long enough," Franz commented as she set it down, his eyes suddenly loaded with suspicion.

"Sorry," she said as she walked around the table to take in her position behind Pascale and started rubbing his shoulders.

"Actually, we don't need you. Scram," Franz rudely dismissed her.

"Did I do something wrong? I'll be quicker with the drinks next time, I promise," she rambled.

"There's not going to be a next time. Now leave us alone and go wait on your tables. I'll deal with you when I'm done. Go on!"

Ana didn't waste any time and ran away toward the bathroom.

"Stupid girl! I apologize. Now, where were we?"

AWARE of the security cameras outside the office, Jorja kept her face hidden as she entered. Ana had sneaked her into the club via the staff entrance at the rear of the building. She had done what she could in the limited amount of time to obscure her identity and entered disguised as a young man wearing a fake mustache and a cap. Thankfully, they had arrived early and avoided being seen by any of the other girls when Ana seated her at the small table, and, so far, their plan was running smoothly.

The club was busy and it was easy to sneak behind the heavy purple curtain without anyone noticing. She followed the short passage to where the office was at the far end and slipped inside. The workroom was small and cramped, made worse by the enormous cluttered desk that stood in the middle of the room. Her gaze danced throughout the space, searching for the wall that housed the safe. It wasn't hard to find since it was the only wall that wasn't covered by bulky filing cabinets and shelves. Recalling Ana's clue to opening the panel in the wall, Jorja moved in behind the desk and searched for a trigger. The desk was messy, with receipts and ledgers scattered everywhere amongst three mugs of cold coffee and a jar of antacid tablets. There was nothing that stood out as obvious so she crouched down under the desk where she easily found the small button that was stuck to the inside of the desk's frame. When she pushed it, the panel instantly popped open to reveal the safe that was built into the small section of exposed wall directly behind the desk.

She moved quickly, pausing for the briefest of moments to take in the full specifications of the medium sized safe. It was bigger than she had assumed, but, as initially predicted, it was a permutation lock—second generation, if she had to be exact. Twenty years ago, it took less than thirty seconds for her to crack one of those. But it had been a long time since then and nerves suddenly made her doubt if she could still do it.

She anchored her hands on the safe, drew in two deep breaths to focus her mind, and asked God to help her. But, feelings of guilt almost instantly came over her for having asked God to contribute to her sinful act. As if it was just to ask someone so holy and righteous to sin on her behalf. She was breaking the law and deep in her heart she knew what she was about to do would not be condoned by God —nor would it please Him. So instead, she retracted her request and begged God to forgive her instead. Deciding that she'd break the rules on her own and bear whatever consequence came from it, she tried to ignore the raging emotions that tugged at her conscience and threatened to overwhelm her. And, much to her surprise, she succeeded in shrugging it off, pinning her focus on the reasons for doing it in the first place as she quickly set about opening the safe.

With steadied breathing, she closed her eyes and pinned her ear against the cold steel next to the lock, shutting the world and its distractions off. With practiced acute hearing, she focused her senses on the soft clicking that came from inside the safe with each gentle rotation of the dial. When the first bolt retracted, marking the successful unlocking of the first number in the sequence, she stopped, then rotated the dial in the opposite direction. It was as if her body ran on auto, calling to mind with sharp precision exactly what she had done so many times before. There were five numbers in total and she set about it in trancelike state, unlocking each one with ease. When the final number retracted the last bolt in the wheel-lock, the door sprung open, and energy surged through her body like a bolt of lightning.

She had done it. She had cracked the safe. She was one step closer to finding the painting, to freeing Ben, to finally being rid of her past.

But euphoria had distracted her, or perhaps it was pride that had caused her to momentarily lose track of the time. And when voices from the narrow corridor on the other side of the office door suddenly jerked her from her daze, it took nearly all her strength to hold back the panic it now sent into her limbs.

CHAPTER SEVENTEEN

Adrenaline pushed her body into motion and her hands moved swiftly through the contents of the safe. Stacks of crisp, new notes, neatly bundled by denomination, took up most of the space, nearly fully concealing the three paper folders that stood flush against one of the walls of the safe.

Aware of the voices drawing closer, she barely breathed, her heart pounding in her ears. With shaky hands she pulled out all three folders and tucked them inside her waistband beneath her shirt, not stopping to search its contents. There was no time, she had to get out, and fast.

Slamming the safe's door back in place, she turned the dial several times to cover her tracks, then raced back to the button beneath the desk. Adrenaline turned her legs to a wobbly mess and she nearly stumbled and met with the floor. But she managed to control her balance and triggered the panel back into position a split second before the office door opened. Surprised by the intrusion, she fell down on her knees and hid behind the desk.

"Jorja, it's me. Are you in here?" Ana's voice whispered into the space and pulled Jorja to her feet.

"Hurry! He's on his way back!" Ana urged, her head being the only part of her body that was visible inside the doorframe.

Jorja raced toward the exit, briefly looking over her shoulder with a final sweep of the office, ensuring she hadn't left any evidence behind.

"This way!" Ana ushered her toward a storage closet halfway down the passage.

"You can't leave through the main lounge now. He's hovering by the bar. Quick, hide in here," she urged, unlocking the storage room's door. "Tell me you got it," she added last minute.

"I did," Jorja smiled.

Franz's voice came from behind the purple curtain.

"Hurry!" she said while pushing Jorja through the barely open door as she grabbed two rolls of loo paper from the closest shelf.

"WHY AREN'T you out there, serving your tables?" Franz's voice roared directly behind her, just as Ana locked the door back in place.

"Just getting some more toilet rolls." She gave her sweetest smile to win him over.

"Why? That's not your job? Your job is to keep the customers happy and get them drunk so they can spend more money." His eyes suddenly narrowed, recalling the warning he'd received from Pascale. "Or are you hiding something?"

"No, don't be silly. Like I said, I just came to fetch more—"

"Yeah, yeah, hand over the key. I don't believe you. Something tells me you are up to no good."

He pushed her out of the way and yanked the key from her hand, jamming it into the lock.

Ana shivered as panic ran through her veins, her mind working frantically at a way to stop him from going into the storage room.

"Jürgen's dead," she said, forcing tears to her eyes. "I just needed time to cry, away from the customers."

Franz paused and looked back at her.

"I know, big deal, the guy was a rat. Crying's not going to bring him back. The way I see it, you should be working harder now that there's no one to pay your bills for you. So, get out there and do what I'm paying you to do!"

His callous voice made her tremble and she froze on

the spot. Unable to rescue herself, much less Jorja, from the dire situation she now found herself in.

"What are you waiting for, girl? Get back to work or you're fired!"

Now, hot under the collar, Franz's normally light pink skin was suddenly bright red. Abandoning his efforts to open the storage closet, he pushed down the short corridor instead and disappeared into his office.

Ana stood waiting in front of the storage room, suddenly realizing he had taken the key with him.

She tried the handle first, but the door was locked then rapped her fingers lightly on the door as she placed her mouth against the seam of the doorpost.

"Jorja, he's gone. He took the key," she whispered. "I'll be back with the spare in a bit, okay? Stay quiet."

She didn't wait for an answer back and hastily went in search of the spare key. But when she returned less than five minutes later, key in hand, she unlocked the door and found Jorja was no longer there.

JORJA'S slim body slithered stealthily through the tight air duct. Despite Ana's best efforts to lure Franz away, she had initially thought she wouldn't make it into the roof in time before he would barge in to catch her. But miraculously, she had managed to escape undetected. With no blueprint of the building, she continued to snake her way along the dusty duct that clearly hadn't ever been cleaned, reasoning that it was her best chance of getting out of the building without being seen.

With nothing but the small light from her mobile phone's screen illuminating the way, one foot of light at a time, her progress was slow. But besides the darkness and thick layers of dust challenging her escape, she soon encountered a challenge far worse. A few yards into the duct, the dim light shone directly into the red eyes of the largest rat she had ever seen. Unable to avoid it, the rodent crawled over her hand and disappeared into the darkness somewhere at her feet. It made her skin crawl, shuddering as it ran past her, and she muffled her unavoidable squeals in the crook of her arm as it did so. Fear of encountering more rats, she pushed harder, propelling her body through the duct as if she was being chased. When she turned left at a junction, stopping briefly to catch her breath, she realized when she could no longer feel the club's music pulsing beneath her body, that she was in the clear.

At the next vent, she peered through the slats first and saw several crates of food in the room below that appeared to be a pantry. She dropped down into the space, pausing to take in her surroundings.

In the distance she could hear kitchen noises mingled with faint talking. She popped her head around the wall of the open pantry and spotted the kitchen on the far end to her right, and an exit door directly to her left. Her heart leaped with joy and she wasted no time to dash toward it, elated to find it opening up to a narrow alley.

Her feet hit the scattered puddles, splashing water up behind her as she ran to where the dark alley ended in what she knew was the street in front of the club.

Taking little notice of the man smoking a cigarette, his back facing hers as he leaned against the corner where the street met the alley, she slowed to a brisk walk, ditching the fake mustache and cap in the dumpster next to her before she passed him and turned up into the street at the opposite corner. Crossing the road she made her way to where Ana had left her little yellow car a block away, deciding she'd stop there to make a call and let her know she had managed to get out alive.

But, in the quiet night air, footsteps suddenly echoed close behind her. She walked a little faster and listened if the strides increased in speed also.

It did.

Perhaps someone had seen her, or maybe it was just Ana, so she popped a quick glance over her shoulder and saw that it was the man who had stood smoking his cigarette. Her heart pushed into her throat. Perhaps she had underestimated the club's security. Why else would he be following her? Not wanting to find out, she crossed to the other side of the road.

He did the same.

She increased her pace.

He did so too.

Fear suddenly pushed into her stomach as she realized the stranger was chasing after her. Once more she crossed into one of the adjoining streets, away from Ana's car, and set into a slow jog.

But once again, the man did the same.

She turned to assess his distance. He was too close, so she ran faster, now putting in every effort to lose him. His feet hit the concrete sidewalk, sounding louder with each stride he took.

He wasn't giving up.

She darted into a sideways alley and sped towards an iron gate. It was locked. Frantic she searched for another way out, but there was none.

Adrenaline surged into her long limbs and pushed her up the high fence. Behind her, the man yelled for her to stop. His voice sounded somewhat familiar, but she kept climbing.

When he had reached the fence, she felt his strong hand close around her ankle, pulling her down toward him.

She fought back, kicking to free her leg, dragging her body higher up the fence.

"Who are you and what did you do at the club?" the man demanded.

She knew that voice and turned to look.

Even in the shadows of the dark alley, their eyes locked and they instantly recognized each other.

"You?" Pascale's voice came at her.

Jorja felt his grip ease around her ankle, and using the opportunity to her advantage, shoved her other boot into his hand. The handsome man she'd instantly recognized from the night outside the church, cringed and let go of her foot, allowing her to climb her way to freedom as she disappeared into the darkness over the fence.

CHAPTER EIGHTEEN

It was close to two in the morning when Ana finally exited the club. Doubt had gnawed at her insides all night long and by the time she stepped outside, she was ready to break down in tears. Unable to get away sooner and forced to work her full shift, she had managed to stifle the lingering concerns that had slowly but steadily escalated throughout the night. But, whilst keeping her mind off Jürgen's death was hard, keeping herself convinced that Jorja hadn't conned her, proved to be much harder. And, the more she allowed her emotions to get the better of her, the more she realized she really didn't know anything about the woman who had mysteriously appeared on her doorstep when she was at her most vulnerable. She had blindly trusted her, given her everything she and Jürgen had lived for and planned, and now she had run off into the sunset that was meant for them instead.

She knew Franz hadn't caught her, which made not knowing where she was so much worse. Yet, as Ana walked away from the club, she clung to the tiniest flicker of hope that refused to be snuffed by her persistent paranoia. She had looked in Jorja's eyes and seen integrity behind her words. There was sincerity to her cause—and the cash to support it. With newfound hope, Ana now bolted for her car, her eyes wide and expectant of seeing Jorja waiting patiently somewhere nearby in the shadows. But when she reached her little yellow car, Jorja wasn't there either. Disappointment sank into her limbs and she slammed her bag down atop her car's hood. Anger welled up inside her and she cursed inward at her credulous stupidity while she reached inside her bag in search of her car keys.

Behind her, a sudden sense of someone present had her quickly turn around, expecting with every last drop of hope she still had within her, to find Jorja. But as her eyes adjusted to the figure that walked toward her, she was ill prepared to see that it hadn't been Jorja who had been waiting for her.

Stunned to see Pascale's handsome face come into view from behind her car, she stumbled back against her door and dropped her keys beside her feet.

"You gave me a fright," she smiled, her voice laced with a mixture of fear and curiosity as she stooped to collect her keys.

He stepped toward her, his presence intimidating and intrusive all at once.

"Can I help you with something?" she dared to ask, the car keys clinging between her trembling fingers.

"That depends."

She tried reading the tone behind his words and quickly answered.

"Oh, I don't do that, but if you want I can get Joleen to—"

"I'm not interested in that. I think you know why I'm here."

A dry lump bottled in her throat and she forced it back down. "Not really, no, I don't."

Her voice didn't convince Pascale who allowed the lingering silence to repeat his question on his behalf.

His reticence made her uncomfortable and she deflected by flirting with him instead.

"We could go back inside for another drink if you want?"

She traced the lapel of his expensive suit as she said it and he snatched her hand, gripping it hard beneath his fingers.

"You're hurting me!"

"Speak, I don't have all night."

She squealed as he squeezed harder, pushing her against the door of her car.

"Honestly, I don't know what you're talking about. Please, let me go!"

It went against every grain in Pascale's body with what he was about to do but it was the only way to get her to talk. His strong hand circled her small neck while the other retrieved a pocket-sized switchblade from inside his coat. Pressing it against the boney curves of her cheek, his eyes stern and threatening, he asked again.

"Tell me about the woman. Why was she in the club?"

Ana's eyes were wide, her body paralyzed with fear as he pinned her against the car. Jorja was nowhere to be seen and for all she knew, she'd taken off with the cash she had promised—and the painting. There was no way of knowing if she were to be trusted. But what she did know without any doubt, was that she wasn't prepared to die for her. Still, despite the uncertainty that tormented her heart and mind, the ache and desperation to find her and Jürgen's paradise was stronger. She wanted to believe, needed to believe every promise Jorja had made. She was her last hope and her only way out of the life she had now become trapped in. Deciding to take one more chance at bluffing her way out of Pascale's tyranny, she answered.

"What woman? I don't know who you're talking about."

"Don't mess with me, Ana. Unless you want to end up dead like your fiancé."

Panic ripped through Ana's petite body as the weight of his words snuffed every grain of hope and she knew she wasn't going to win this fight. Forced into confession, she allowed the words to roll off her tongue.

"I don't know much about her. She knew a guy who was in prison with Jürgen."

"What's her name?"

"Jorja."

"And who's the cellmate she claims to know?"

"I can't remember."

"Try harder."

Tears ran down Ana's cheek.

"Honestly, I can't remember. It was a weird name, but it doesn't matter anyway. He's dead."

Her words momentarily silenced Pascale. But as her body tried to relax out of his grip, his arm pinned her against the car once more.

"Why was she in the club?"

Ana hesitated and his hand tightened around her neck.

"She broke into Franz's safe."

"So she stole money?"

For the swiftest of moments Ana thought of letting him believe that. It could be the lifeline she needed for him to let her go. And, staring into Pascale's eyes she almost thought she would get away with it too. But then his eyes suddenly narrowed and once again pushed her into a corner from which she knew she couldn't escape.

"You're hiding something. What else was in the safe?"

She hesitated a tad longer than she had intended to and Pascale drove the tip of his knife deeper into her cheek until the tiniest droplet of blood escaped and wet her cheek.

"The painting! It's about the stupid painting," Ana said, the tears now freely flowing down her face.

The frown between Pascale's brows told her he was

confused about her disclosure and, fearing he'd kill her, she quickly told him more.

"She's after the painting. The one with Jesus, painted by the *Mona Lisa* guy. Apparently, some evil client or something is blackmailing her into getting it for him. That's all I know, I swear!"

Pascale held his position as he digested what he had just learned.

"And what did Franz have to do with it? What did she think she'd find in the safe?"

"He had everything to do with it. The sleazeball had my Jürgen steal the painting and then let him take the fall for him while he cashed in and got bumped up the line in the *Gardiens*."

Again, Pascale took his time taking in the information.

"You're hurting me. Please? I've told you everything I know. Please don't kill me too."

He eased his grip, just a tad to allow more oxygen into her timid body.

"So this woman broke into Franz's safe to steal what exactly? The painting?"

"No, the painting isn't in Europe, it's in Abu Dhabi. Franz kept the address or something locked in his safe. I swear, that's all I know."

Pascale studied her face but her eyes had confirmed she was telling him the truth. He buried the knife back inside his coat, then released her from his grip.

"Go home, and, Ana, don't breathe a word to Franz about any of this, you got it?"

She nodded quickly, needing no reminding of the threat that lay behind his request. When Pascale turned to walk away, she didn't waste another moment to watch him disappear in the shadowy street he had come from.

Tossing her bag toward the passenger seat, her hand moved quickly to lock her doors before she sped the car to the safety of her home.

———

PASCALE'S HEART raced where he stood in the dark alley watching Ana's yellow car leave. If what Ana had told him was true, the end was closer than he'd thought, and Gerard Dubois was precisely where he needed him to be: worried.

It wasn't hard to piece it all together. Gerard had given it away at the meeting the other evening when he had expressed how much he wanted the *Salvator Mundi*. All this time he had known one of his own had turned on him, but he'd never known who. It must have driven him crazy, not knowing who to trust. And little did he realize that his Judas had been right under his nose all this time.

Excitement made Pascale cry out with joy where he stood alone in the middle of the dark road. A big smile settled on his mouth and he victoriously drove his fist up toward the heavens before his hands cradled the back of his neck. It was the happiest he'd been in nearly a decade of playing this game and soon it would all be over.

At long last he was ahead of Gerard and knowing that, for once, the man had no idea what was playing off behind his back, made his toes curl with glee. As he walked back to where he had parked his car in a nearby parking lot, Pascale couldn't stop smiling. He'd known Gerard for many years and could only imagine how that must have driven him crazy over the years. Having one of his own men steal and sell his painting out from right under him would have made him livid.

And now that he knew what the woman was after, he could use her to do his dirty work for him and bring the painting to him instead. Finally, he had everything he needed to take Gerard Dubois down. Once and for all.

And Ana was the missing link that was going to lead him straight to the mysterious woman who called herself Jorja.

CHAPTER NINETEEN

A na's car roared into her driveway and screeched to a grinding halt. She had been a crying mess behind the wheel and nearly drove off the road a few times.

Eager to get out of the car and flee toward the safety of her home, she stumbled out of the car and fell to her knees, sending the contents of her bag to scatter across the uneven paving. The commotion set several dogs off on a barking frenzy that had the neighbors quickly turn their porch lights on in response. Not wanting to face the prying questions, she hastily scooped the spilled items back into her bag and made her way around the rear of the house.

The house was dark and quiet since her two house-mates were both working the night shift at the nearby hospital. Before she had met Jürgen, the three of them had studied nursing together, a career she was happy to do for the rest of her life. But once Jürgen was released from prison, keeping her job at the hospital became a challenge.

She had allowed him to pump her head full of pipe dreams about living with him on an island paradise somewhere far away. Unrealistic dreams she now knew only existed in his head.

As she fumbled with the keys in the lock, a twig snapped in the hedge behind her and she spun around to see what had caused it. But the small hedged in garden seemed undisturbed so she turned her attention back to getting inside her home.

When the back door that led into her kitchen finally unlocked, she slammed it shut behind her and dropped her bag onto the floor by her feet, sinking down in a blubbering pile next to it on the floor. Letting the darkness cocoon her, she sobbed her heart out. Able to mourn her fiancé's death for the first time since it happened, she finally let go of all the hurt and tension the horrible night had delivered. She regretted ever falling in love with Jürgen, for letting him mess up her life and leaving her behind to pick up the broken pieces. For betraying him when she told the man from the club what he had planned. And for allowing a stranger to swindle her into thinking she could make it all go away.

Caught up in her distress, she didn't hear the soft footsteps that had walked toward and stopped next to her, until Jorja's voice whispered right beside her.

"Ana, it'll be all right," she said gently.

Her unexpected presence startled Ana into panic and sent her crawling to safety to the other side of the kitchen.

"It's okay! Ana, it's me, Jorja."

Ana scrambled to her feet and moved to switch on the light.

"No, leave it off, it's safer that way," Jorja cautioned.

"How did you get in?" Ana eventually managed, instantly realizing the stupidity of her question. "Of course, you are used to breaking into places."

"Sorry, I didn't mean to scare you, and yes, I shouldn't have broken into your house. But with all that has happened in the street, the neighbors are on edge and I couldn't risk them seeing us together."

"It's fine." Ana walked over to Jorja so she could see her face in the dim moonlight that beamed through the nearby window. "I thought you had left me behind."

"Leave you! Why would I do that? I made you a promise and I intend on keeping it, Ana."

Ana's shoulders slackened in relief.

"You mean that?"

"Absolutely. I couldn't do this without you. I told you already. I know all there is to know about wanting to turn your life around."

A faint smile broke on Ana's young face. "Did you get what you wanted then?"

Ana turned to grab two sodas from the refrigerator.

"And some!"

Jorja's answer brought a frown to Ana's face, asking Jorja to explain.

"Come see." Jorja nudged her toward the cozy sitting room where she had been poring over the folders she took from the safe. She had spread the open folders onto the coffee table, illuminated by a small night lamp she had found in one of the bedrooms.

"What's all this?"

"This, my dear Ana, is our ticket to freedom."

The blank expression on Ana's face invited her to tell her more.

"It seems Franz has a few secrets that, from what I can tell, will land him in quite a bit of trouble if his boss finds out. Not only do I now know for certain that he was responsible for intercepting the *Salvator Mundi*, but, I also have a full record of every other art heist he had pulled. And from the looks of it, they weren't ordered by the *Gardiens*."

Ana took a seat next to her and glanced at the papers that lay in an unorganized mess atop the table.

"How do you know this? I can't make out anything that's written on these papers. It's just a bunch of jumbled words and cartoons."

"Precisely the point—they're cryptic messages with what looks like schematics. Look, I'm no genius when it comes to codebreaking, but I am dead sure what heist schematics looks like. It might take me a while to figure the others out, but for now, this one will do."

She held out one of the sheets of paper and sank back in the couch. "This one is the only one we need to concern ourselves with."

"Why?"

"Because, Ana, it's everything I need to know on where to find the *Salvator Mundi*."

Ana studied the piece of paper. "Looks like a bunch of garbage doodling to me, but okay, I'll take your word for it. Now what?"

Jorja took the piece of paper, buried it inside its folder, and tidied up the rest of the papers.

"Now we get some sleep and tomorrow morning, I'll tell you where to meet my contact who will fix you up with a new passport. It will be ready in fifteen minutes. You can trust him, he's already created your new identity. I've also set up an appointment for you at the bank where you will use your passport to access the money I've left for you in a safety deposit box. By the time the bank has completed the transfer into your new account, my contact will have already booked you a one-way ticket to an undisclosed location where you can make a fresh start. All you need to do is pack a small carry on, he'll take care of the rest."

Ana stared at Jorja, her eyes wide and bewildered. "Just like that?"

"Just like that."

"But, what about my friends? I can't just leave without saying goodbye."

Jorja placed a gentle hand on Ana's shoulder. "It's not

going to be easy, Ana, take it from me. It will be the hardest thing you'll ever do. But, if you want a new start, to stay alive, you're going to have to put everything you know behind you and not look back, ever."

New tears welled in Ana's sad eyes.

"What about you, and your friend? The painting?" she said.

"I'll be okay. I have what I need, and, if all goes according to plan, I should have my friend back by this time next week. Now, go on and get some rest. Tomorrow is the start of the brand new life you and Jürgen had been dreaming of."

BUT, an hour later, Jorja still tossed and turned on the couch Ana had made up for her in the sitting room. She had pretended not to be scared, to have it all together and under control, for Ana's sake. But in truth, she had never been more afraid in all her life. Yes, she had found out who had bought the stolen painting, and even the name of the city he lived in, but, in all the jobs she'd pulled in her once illustrious career as an international art thief, had she ever been more ill prepared, or forced to work alone.

Having finally given up the fight to sleep, she sat up and opened the folder that had all the information on the *Salvator Mundi's* location. She left the light off, flipping the loose sheets back and forth in an almost meditative state as if it could somehow calm her nerves. When the action had no effect, she tossed it back onto the table, watching as it fell face down on top of the rest of the folders. In the pale light her eye lingered on a partial etching that was on the back of a small piece of paper that had slipped out and she hadn't before paid much attention to. At first, she didn't realize what she was looking at, but moments later her brain had caught up and she lunged toward the paper. Yanking it out from the folder, she reached for the night lamp, turning the design to see it fully.

There was no denying it. She had seen it before, twice, in fact. The design on the paper between her fingers matched the tattoo she'd seen on the wrist of the handsome stranger she'd run into outside the church. Then, once again, when he had grabbed a hold of her ankle when she escaped and fled from the club.

CHAPTER TWENTY

J orja's heart pounded against her chest. At once even more anxious than before, she jumped to her feet and started pacing the area around the table. She had searched through the contents of the other two folders and found the same design stamped into the paper fibers on the back of each of the folders. It was small and color-less, which was no wonder she hadn't noticed it initially.

Lord, what have I gotten myself into? What have I gotten Ana into? Her prayers echoed in her fatigued mind while fear once again threatened to squeeze the life out of her heart and soul. If the logo belonged to the *Gardiens*, it meant the unknown man was one of them, and by now he might very well know exactly what she was planning. Hanging around might be the worst thing she could do, especially if, by now, Franz had discovered that the files had gone missing from his safe. He'd instantly know it was Ana since he had made his suspicions of her clear when he found her at the storage closet instead of working her tables.

Jorja snuck a watchful eye from behind the curtains out into the street. For all she knew they were already prowling outside getting ready to kill them. She lingered there for a bit, searching between the houses, the shrubs, the cars. But everything was dark and undisturbed. She bounced nervously between two more windows, paying attention to each of the parked cars up and down the street. None of them seemed out of place and she knew most of the vehicles had been parked in the same spot since before Ana came home. But then one of the vehicles caught her interest and she honed in on it, suddenly uncertain if it had been there earlier. A nearby tree cast a dark shadow across the windshield and obscured the car's interior, making it difficult to see if anyone was inside. Paying better attention to the style and model of the car, she thought it was too expensive to belong to anyone in that neighborhood and she fought hard not to let the anxious feeling in the pit of her stomach overwhelm her. She fell back behind the curtain, thought on it a bit, then moved to grab a better view from a side window. Barely visible she made out the silhouette of a person sitting behind the wheel. A chilling feeling ran down her spine. Whoever was inside that car was staking out the house, she was certain of it.

Pushing herself away from the window, she made her way down the small corridor toward Ana's room, but paused outside the door, unable to bring herself to wake the poor girl only to frighten her even more. If whoever was in that car was the man from the church, the man who had seen Jorja escape from the club and chased her through the streets, then it was safe to guess he wasn't there for Ana anyway.

With newfound clarity, Jorja concluded that it was best she parted ways with Ana. The longer she stayed with her, the higher the risk on Ana's life. All the poor girl did was fall in love with the wrong man. She didn't deserve paying for it with her life. Besides, by morning, Ana will get what she needs to start over. Time wasn't standing still. She had Ben to think of first.

Deciding that leaving was her only plausible option, she turned her attention back to the folders on the table. Ripping a blank corner from one of the pieces of paper, she jotted down the details where Ana needed to meet the contact to pick up her passport. Ana had left her handbag on the kitchen counter and Jorja quickly moved to slip the piece of paper into the cigarette box before she scooped the rest of the paper folders together and stuck it neatly inside her waistband, under her shirt.

She had already taken care of everything Ana would need, and a quick message to Andre would have his runner help her with the rest.

When she opened the kitchen door to sneak out the back, it creaked noisily and Jorja prayed that neither Ana nor the neighboring dogs had woken up from it. If she could jump over the hedge into the yard of the house behind, she could sneak out their garden gate and avoid being seen by the watchman out front.

A quick inspection of the six-feet high hedge allowed her to find her first foothold and she began to climb. The thick foliage concealed the spiky thorns beneath its leaves, making her flinch as her hands took a hold of the webbed branches. She drove her body higher with her legs, pulling the sleeves of her jacket over her hands to protect them. Once she had reached the top, she paused to scan the dark backyard for signs of any dogs. When she thought it safe to proceed, she dropped down into the yard and bolted toward the small, rusty gate in the far corner. Grateful it stood ajar just enough for her to squeeze through without causing the rusty hinges to squeak, she made it to the other side and ran out into the dark, quiet street.

PASCALE SUDDENLY FOUND himself restless where he sat waiting behind the wheel of his car. He had parked it a few houses away from Ana's house after he'd raced after her and followed her home. Admittedly, he had secretly hoped she would scoop the mystery woman up along the way, but she hadn't. Instead, she hadn't moved from her home since she screeched the car into her driveway. He had watched for lights in the windows, even slunk around to the back of the house in the hopes of sneaking a glimpse inside, but everything had seemed quiet.

His fingers rapped impatiently on the leather-coated steering wheel and he briefly shuffled forward in his seat, eager to ease the cramps in his legs from having sat in the same position most of the night.

Fueled by the insatiable hunger to finish what he had started nearly ten years prior, his mind and body felt more alert than if he had consumed ten cups of coffee. His spirit was restless and he longed to finally put it all to rest, to find peace.

He thought of lighting another cigarette, but quickly abandoned the idea. It was time he quit the nasty habit that he had only started because of it fitting the profile he was forced to assume. He rolled down his window, and drew in the fresh dewy fragrance nature so lavishly provided instead. The air was crisp and inviting. He could do with stretching his legs, he thought, and wasted no time to step out of his car, making sure to shut the door quickly to avoid being seen in the door's small interior light.

The entire neighborhood was in a deep slumber and there was no sign of any life as far as his eyes could see up or down the street. Ana's house also remained entirely covered in darkness. Dawn won't come around for another two hours, and, by the looks of things, she shouldn't be awake anytime before then.

He could do with a small break, he told himself, and decided to head out to the nearby twenty-four hour motor port around the corner. With any luck, they'd have a fresh pot of coffee and something to ease the hunger that had suddenly caught him off guard. Back behind the wheel, he turned the car's nose around, keeping his lights off so as to not wake up the street. He rolled the vehicle slowly down the street and turned left twice until he drove down the road that ran between the rows of houses directly behind Ana's. As he rounded the corner, he spotted a shadow that moved quickly between the tall shrubbery in front of one of the houses. At first he ignored it, assuming it was a feral cat or some other nocturnal animal. But then the shadow became clearer as it dashed across the front lawn and rapidly took on the silhouette of a person. As he focused his eyes, thinking at first it was a burglary in progress, he was soon greeted instead by someone far more familiar.

He swiftly hid his car in the shadows next to the side-walk behind a parked car, and watched in silent disbelief, perplexed over how it was that luck had found him when he had least expected it. It was as if some invisible force had guided him there, intentionally, to catch her sneaking off into the darkness, away from Ana's house.

He hung back and crouched down below the steering wheel, keeping his eyes pinned on the woman's back as she ran away down the street. When she was a reasonably safe distance away from him, he pulled his car out of hiding and, with the headlights still off, quietly trailed her to where, two streets down, he watched her skillfully pick the lock of a nearby car, before she drove the stolen vehicle toward the city.

CHAPTER TWENTY-ONE

Jorja left the stolen vehicle outside her hotel and hurriedly made her way to her room. Guilt over having had to steal a car had haunted her all the way there. She didn't want to fall back into sin. All she wanted was to do what she needed as quickly and cleanly as possible. Her mind had been held hostage by evil images of Ben being tortured and all she wanted to do was rescue him. Time was fast running out, and with only four days left, she was faced with the impossible. But, with Ana safely taken care of and out of the way, she could now focus on getting to Abu Dhabi and coming up with a plan to steal the *Salvator Mundi*.

In the safety of her bedroom, her fingers dialed Andre's phone.

"Yo, girl, do you have any idea what time it is?" His voice croaked on the other end of the phone.

It wasn't that early—6 a.m.—but Andre 'Mad Dog's' business hours were nocturnal.

"There's been a change of plans, sorry," Jorja said.

"There always is with you, Gigi. What's up, fam?"

"I can't be there with Ana to pick up the passport and the money. I need your guy to see it through, get her where she needs to be."

She heard rustling that sounded like Andre was sitting up in his bed.

"Why? What's going on?"

"I can't risk her getting caught, that's all. Just please take care of her for me, will you?"

"If you're in trouble, Gigi, tell me! I can help. You're running out of time and there ain't no way you can do this on your own. You've never pulled a job alone, especially not one this big. I have a bad feeling about this one, Gigi, please, let me make a few calls. I know a couple of—"

"I'll be fine, Andre, please, I have to do this my way. Just help the girl, okay?" She could have added that she needed to do it God's way, but Andre wasn't ready to hear how she was transforming. All that mattered now was that she got the job done without jeopardizing her newfound relationship with God. She wanted to do right by him, yearned for his grace and absolution.

She ended the call and moved to open the small drawer of the bedside table, using the edges as leverage to snap the burner phone in half. As it broke, one half slipped inside the drawer and she yanked it open to take it out. In the back of the drawer, tucked away into one of the corners, she spotted a thin, black Bible, the small sticker on the front noting it had been provided by an organization called Gideons. She quickly snatched it up, hugging it against her chest as fear suddenly tugged hard at the hollows of her heart.

It was as if God had just given her the sign she needed.

Her stomach turned and weighed down her chest as she thought about the task that lay ahead. A task she knew she wasn't prepared for. Overwhelmed with dread, tears blurring her vision, she whispered a prayer.

"God, if you can hear me, please help me do this. Help me get Ben back. I'm scared and I don't know if I can do this. I know I haven't known you for long, but Ewan always told me that all I needed to do was ask. So I'm asking, God. I can't do this alone. Thank you. Amen."

She sat clutching the Bible for a moment or two longer before she slipped it back inside the drawer. Wiping away her tears, she took a deep meditative breath and refocused her mind on her mission. From the concealed base in her luggage, she swapped out the contents for the paper folders she'd stolen from Franz's office, once more memorizing the painting's location before she locked the suitcase and rolled it across the floor next to the door.

Hoping the items in her ensemble of tools were all she needed to pull off the heist, she checked through each one before transferring it into the silver studded black leather belt-bag Andre had cleverly included amongst the clothing items he'd left her. The compartments were just large enough to fit all the items he'd so carefully picked out for her: a pair of black gloves, a set of lock picks, sunglasses, and a digital code grabbing device. This time, however, she decided to include the small pearl-handle pistol, just in case. She finished it off with a wad of cash and her fake passport.

Feeling as prepared as she'd ever be, she scanned the room once more, grabbed her luggage and made her way down to the lobby.

"GOOD MORNING, mademoiselle, I was just about to send someone up to your room. This came for you." The friendly desk clerk handed her a plain, sealed envelope.

"Thank you. Who left it?"

"I'm not sure, mademoiselle. It arrived with this morning's newspapers. The driver said someone handed it to him outside and asked to make sure you got it."

"He asked for me by name?"

"No, mademoiselle, but you're the only one who fit his description. May I ask, is everything okay?"

Jorja buried the envelope inside her jacket's pocket.

"Yes, yes, thank you. I'd like to check out though, please? I'll be back to collect my luggage. Could you please make sure it's kept in lockup until I'm back? Under the strictest security, please."

She had planned on taking it with but her instincts

told her not to. She had left Franz's folders in the concealed base. A sharp feeling of caution had come over her and keeping it safe was now more important than ever. She was certain, once deciphered, the contents would deliver far more than meets the eye, and if it was what she was suspecting it to be, she could use it as collateral, to free herself, or Ben—or both of them!

"Of course. I will personally take care of it, mademoiselle. It was a pleasure to have you stay with us. I hope everything was to your satisfaction?"

"It was, thank you."

She watched as he sealed the suitcase, added a note to it, and locked the piece of luggage inside the small lockup room before she moved away to read the letter. Standing to one side, she took out the envelope and tore it open, glancing over her shoulder when she got the sense that she might be watched.

The single sheet of paper simply read: Tick-Tock. Below it, a large drop of blood was smeared across the paper.

Ben's blood! The thought sent icy chills down her spine as soon as she'd realized that Sokolov was responsible for sending the letter. In usual fashion it was a not so subtle reminder that he was watching her every move. His way of making sure she understood what was at stake if she didn't deliver on the promise she'd made him. As if she needed reminding that he was holding Ben captive.

Her fist closed over the letter, crumpling it into a

compressed ball before she tossed it into the rubbish bin outside the hotel's entrance. Newfound urgency surged through her body and once again, fear tortured her soul.

SOON AFTER SHE had left the hotel, the taxi dropped her at the airport where she booked the next flight to Abu Dhabi. Miraculously she had managed to secure a direct flight, shortening her flight time to only six hours. Aware that she wouldn't make it through the customs X-ray machine carrying the contents of her hip bag, she scanned the terminal for another solution. If there was one thing she had learned a very long time ago, then it was to always think three steps ahead. A plan was only a plan if it was successful, and until that happened, it was simply a dance of opportunity.

Her eyes scanned through the rest of the passengers who were also in line waiting to proceed through the customs checkpoint. She searched for a way to get her bag onto the plane without having to go through the scanner, but found none. In the past, Ben would have jammed the scanner, or they'd have someone on the inside. This time, however, she had no one to help her. Panic started to set in as another three passengers moved up the line. Showing no outward signs of her now racing heart, she continued looking for a way out. Then she spotted it: a young boy, waiting nearby with his parents. The boy was in a wheelchair, his body worn out from cancer. To his right, his parents stood talking to the airline staff, filling out last minute paperwork before they'd be taken onboard the plane through a separate entrance. Dangling from the back of his wheelchair was a large green backpack, shaped like a dinosaur. Its body sturdy and large enough to easily conceal her body bag. She dropped out of the line and passed directly behind the boy, nabbing the bag as she walked past. She had worked quickly, like the trained hands of a pickpocket, concealing it under her jacket as she disappeared inside the nearby washroom. Once inside, she removed her body bag and quickly concealed it inside the boy's bag. As swiftly as before, the passengers entirely oblivious to her skilled handiwork, she slipped the bag back over the boy's chair and returned to the line to wait her turn.

CHAPTER TWENTY-TWO

Adrenaline quickened her pulse as she watched the ground staff escort the boy and his parents through a separate boarding entrance, her eyes glued to the green dinosaur dangling from his wheelchair. For a minute or two, she lost sight of them where a wall blocked a clean line of sight. But then they popped up on the other side of the glass door, walking the short distance across the airfield to where they were helped onto the aircraft.

Relieved that her bag had made it onto the plane, Jorja waited her turn and soon made it safely through the security scanner before she too boarded the airplane.

Her seat was several rows behind where they had seated the boy, his wheelchair—with the green backpack —folded away to one side near the flight attendant's station at the front of the plane. She'd have to move quickly, while the passengers were still settling in, she thought out her plan to retrieve her bag.

A friendly flight attendant stood close to the chair, greeting the passengers as they took their seats ahead of her. Laser focused on the challenge that lay in front of her, Jorja continued along the aisle, intentionally passing her seat as she headed to the front of the plane. A frown settled across the hostess' brow.

"Are you having trouble finding your seat, ma'am?"

"No, I think the gentleman seated over there might have trouble breathing. He looks rather uncomfortable, if you ask me." Jorja pointed toward an elderly man who'd already taken his seat in the middle of the plane. His head was bowed since he was reading the inflight safety procedures, but from where they stood, the hostess couldn't tell.

As expected, the red-lipped woman responded quickly, giving Jorja the perfect opportunity to recover her bag. And, since most of the passengers were still standing in the aisle loading their hand luggage in the overhead compartments, she executed her task with ease.

As she shuffled back to her seat, her fanny pack now back where it belonged around her waist, she looked forward to the flight. Without threat, she'd have the time she so desperately needed, to work up a plan to steal the painting.

. . .

BUT, three hours into the flight, Jorja was no closer to finding a foolproof way to steal the painting. Without blueprints, security surveillance, or, most importantly, a solid getaway in place, it was entirely futile and supremely ignorant of her to think she could pull it off and make it out of Abu Dhabi alive. Andre was right, she couldn't do it, not without help.

Resting her head back against her seat, her eyes closed to shut out the distractions around her, she once again asked—no, pleaded—for God to help her. Feeling hopeless and afraid, defeated before she'd even begun, lost in fervent conversation with the one she'd thought would come through for her, Jorja succumbed to the emotions that pushed beyond all reason.

OVERCOME BY A SENSE OF LONELINESS, fear, and the reality that she was destined to fail at rescuing Ben, her body responded in panic. She loosened the seat belt, suddenly feeling claustrophobic as if the aircraft's walls were closing in on her. Tears lay shallow, her throat suddenly tight and constricted, her breathing labored to erratic spurts. Sick built up in her stomach and she launched herself from her seat in search of the toilet. When she burst through the narrow folding door, and shut it behind her, she emptied her stomach, crying as she tried to rid her body from the torment that now saturated her every cell. All she ever wanted was to start a new life, to walk away from the wrong she had done, and to protect Ben from the poor decisions of her past. Instead, her selfish desire to make Züber and Sokolov pay for Ewan's death had clouded her judgement and instead, made it all worse. And now Ben was paying the ultimate price and there was nothing she could do to stop it.

Regret filled her and she wished with all her heart she had trusted Ewan, told him the truth instead. He would have helped her, protected her, just like he'd always promised he would. And though she could have never loved him the way he'd always hoped she would, at least he would have still been alive. At least she wouldn't be there, puking over a toilet on a flight to her own demise. They could have made it work; she could have tried. And Ben would still be alive in the safe haven she'd intentionally left behind for him when she walked out on him all those years ago.

WHEN LIGHT RAPPING on the door jerked her focus away from the self-pity that seemed to have engulfed her entirely, she peeled herself off the floor and leaned back against the wall.

"One minute, please," she spoke through the door, her voice crackly as she hovered over the wash basin to wash her face.

But, as she studied her reflection in the small mirror, saw her swollen, red eyes and the defeat that had settled deep inside her soul, she knew it would take a lot more to heal the brokenness that had now firmly taken root in her heart. By the time she made it back to her seat, she noticed the young girl who sat next to her had settled into another seat a few rows to the front. Relieved to now have the space all to herself, she moved over into the window seat. As she watched the young girl get cozy with a lad roughly the same age as she, Jorja couldn't help thinking that she was wise to get as far away from her as possible. Once again, the small, whispering voices echoed in the dark corners of her mind, tormenting her with guilt over destroying everyone she crossed paths with. It was as if the words were etched deep inside her soul and somehow knew to only surface during the times her spirit felt most crushed.

Exhausted, she leaned her head against the small porthole as she watched the clouds float peacefully underneath the plane. She wondered if this was what Heaven looked like and if God sat somewhere on an enormous gold cloud, watching His creation from His throne. Had God even heard her? What if He didn't want to help her or if she had been so ignorant to assume that He'd want to forgive her? What if her sins were too big for Him to wipe away, if He had stopped caring?

Her mind raced through a million questions she didn't have the answers to. She barely knew God, she hadn't had enough time to learn how He'd respond to her yet. Would she ever? Ewan would have known, but she never gave him the chance to tell her.

She thought of Ben and wondered if he knew God. They didn't know each other anymore, it'd been too long since they were together. Things were different now—she'd changed.

"WE HAVE GOT to stop meeting this way." A deep manly voice suddenly spoke directly next to her and ripped her from her spiritually searching thoughts.

When she turned to look, every cell in her body froze in place. At first she thought of getting away from him, but there was something so commanding of his eyes and stature that her limbs willingly succumbed to his power.

"Didn't mean to startle you," he apologized.

Still, she couldn't speak.

He waited, looked her dead in the eye, inviting her to say something, but she couldn't. She watched as he buckled himself in, then called the flight attendant over.

"Scotch on the rocks, please, and bring one for the lady too. Or shall I just call you 'Jorja'?" he said with a playful grin.

Shocked that he had come to know her true identity, Jorja still couldn't speak.

"Fine, I'll give you a minute then," he said as he rested his head on the headrest and shut his eyes. "The way I see it, you're going to have to say something eventually," he continued. "We're still a long ways off from landing and well, there's nowhere to run now, is there?"

She could slap the smirk off his face, she thought, but restrained herself. Instead, composing herself before she spoke, her voice steely and her body rigid, she said, "What do you want?"

His smile widened before he gave her a sideways glance with one eye open, then closed it again.

"What do you want, and how did you find me?" she asked again.

"Oh, now you want to talk, do you?"

"Enough with the silly games," she said, as she suddenly realized she didn't have the slightest idea who he was.

"Must feel awful not to know your opponent. From what I've heard, you're quite the smart one, always a few steps ahead."

Her throat tightened.

The flight attendant popped her head round the back of their seats and held their drinks out to them.

"Will that be all, Monsieur Lupin?"

Lupin! His name is Lupin!

"Yes, thank you."

He pushed his chiseled chin out as he forced Jorja to take the glass of alcohol and proceeded to hold his glass up to signal that he wanted to toast to something.

"To us working together," he said, and took a sip of his beverage.

"Working together? What are you talking about?" Jorja said, stunned.

Once more, his eyes twinkled and his attractive mouth curled into an amused smile. "Oh, I think you know exactly what I'm talking about, Miss Rose. Now, drink up. We have a lot to talk about." He winked and took another sip of his drink.

"I don't drink," she said, setting the plastic glass down on his tray.

"Interesting."

"What is?"

"I just thought all thieves consumed alcohol. You must be a cut above the rest, then."

Her heart just about stopped in her chest. He knew. He knew who she was.

"See, I told you you knew what I was talking about." The twinkle in his eyes was back.

"What do you want?"

"I believe I already told you. I want to work together."

"I work alone." She turned away and faced the window.

"Well, now see, this is where you're going to ruin this little reunion of ours. You don't have much choice in the matter. We want the same thing, and considering I know a whole lot more about you than you do about me, I think I might have a small advantage over you."

"You know nothing about me."

"I know enough," his voice suddenly low. "Like, for example, the fact that you are carrying a gun, and a whole lot of other paraphernalia generally used to pull a heist of some kind."

CHAPTER TWENTY-THREE

Jorja shifted uncomfortably in her seat, unconsciously fiddling with the bag around her waist.

"Oh, don't worry, I won't say a thing. Although, I must give it to you: the way you snuck that little bag of tricks onto this plane was quite genius and so skillfully done too. Of course, one little whisper to the captain and you won't set foot on the Abu Dhabi tarmac, let alone get away with stealing a painting."

Jorja flushed bright red as heat infused her face and her insides felt as if it was going to ignite at any second.

He smiled again, leaning in to whisper close to her ear. She shuffled uncomfortably, caught off guard with his enigmatic presence that sent sweet tingles down her spine.

Where did that come from? Don't drop your guard, Jorja!

"See, I know things about you. You are mine now."

The ambiguity in his voice made her heart skip to where it exploded into a flurry of butterflies inside her stomach. Trying hard to hide the surprising effect he had on her, she snatched the drink off his tray and took two quick swigs of the gold liquid. Who was this man and why did he affect her so much?

"I thought you didn't drink." The look in his eyes was teasing.

But she was ready to deliver a few surprises of her own and she locked eyes with him when she spoke.

"I might have once been the person you're accusing me of, but I want nothing to do with the *Gardiens*."

She waited and read his eyes, certain she spotted the tiniest inkling of surprise behind his mesmerizing gaze before it once more, turned playful.

"So you think you know me now?"

"I know enough about you to say with certainty that I want nothing to do with you or who you work for."

He held her gaze, his eyes once again taunting her into feeling things she hadn't felt in many years, if ever.

"I can see I am going to need to change your opinion of me. And I do so love a challenge, Miss Rose."

Again, she was left feeling like he had won the round.

"Tell you what," he continued. "How about we start over? The name is Pascale Lupin. I believe you might associate better with my wife, Gabrielle Bouvier?"

Jorja felt her face flush bright red in anger at the mention that he had a wife—and one the entire art world knew of and respected. *Stupid woman!* She cursed herself for being so childish in letting him toy with her like that. She wanted desperately to say something, but couldn't find the right words. So, she just nodded.

"So, you've heard of her then? Good, saves me the trouble of going into her entire family credentials and the history of how we met. It's all so boring anyway. Now, tell me about the painting."

Jorja scoffed. "One would think with all your knowledge and *influence* you'd be quicker in your comprehension. So, let me spell it out for you, Mr. Lupin. I am not going to work with you. Not now. Not ever."

The teasing smile was back on his face, his eyes more amused than before.

"I like working with a feisty woman. Your husband must have his hands full."

She was about to blurt out that she wasn't married, but knew he was hinting. Determined not to be trapped in his flirtatious game, she disengaged, shut her eyes and rested her head back, hoping he'd leave her alone if she ignored him.

"Yes, you're absolutely right. We should get some sleep. There will be a lot to take care of once we land. Stealing a painting of this nature is going to require proper planning, not to mention the getaway. Any good art thief will tell you that the getaway is the most important part to get right in any heist. But then, I'm sure I don't need to tell you that. Someone with your experience will have thought of that first, right? Yes, I'm sure you have it all planned out. It's a good thing we're not pressured by any timeline either. Imagine that."

His mocking words left a deliberate trail of temptation that forced her to turn and look at him. Desperate to respond, she searched for the right words, but he had already rested his head back and closed his eyes.

Deciding it was best not to say anything, she attempted to sleep again, but inwardly, his words had left behind a stinging that left her restless and overwhelmed with a fresh wave of anxiety. Jorja wrestled with the truth of what he'd just said. There simply wasn't enough time left for her to plan the heist, much less find a way of escaping with the painting. He was right. She won't make it out of the country alive, much less save Ben.

AS HER THOUGHTS tormented her soul, and trepidation welled up once more, she couldn't help wonder if God had something to do with Pascale being there. What if he was how God was coming to her aid? But as quick as the pondering surfaced, she pushed it aside. There was no way God would bring a man as evil as Pascale into her life, was there?

For the remainder of the flight she was restless knowing that she was sitting next to a man she guessed was part of a powerful organized crime syndicate. And, as she tried to make sense of it all, doubt crept in. He hadn't admitted to being in the *Gardiens* when she called him out on it. Yet, he was there, the night she escaped from the club, and she'd seen his tattoo and the embossing on the folders. They matched.

She tried sneaking a glimpse of his wrist and instead found herself studying his face and clothes. Guessing he was roughly her age, she could understand how it was that he was married to Madame Bouvier. He was handsome, refined, and precisely the type Gabrielle Bouvier would want to be attached to. Voted one of Europe's elite, she was herself an exceptional catch, especially after she inherited her father's entire fortune.

"You know, you could just ask me and I'll tell you," he said, his eyes still closed.

He had caught Jorja by surprise again, leaving her to wonder anew why he was causing her to act so foolishly around him.

She stuttered a reply. "Ask you what, exactly?"

"How it is that I'm married to a woman like her."

"Who?" She blurted out, once again left baffled over how he knew her thoughts.

He sat up and turned in his seat to face her. "Fine, you win, I'll tell you."

"I didn't ask."

"You didn't have to." The look in his eyes was mischievous.

"Honestly, I have no desire to know. Who you are and who you are married to is none of my concern."

But his voice was gentle and filled with sincerity when he spoke.

"The painting belongs to her family, Jorja. All I want is to get it back to her, where it belongs, that's all. Now, if it's about the money, I have plenty, and I'll pay you handsomely. But, I happen to know it's not about the money, but about your husband being in some kind of trouble."

Realizing he'd somehow cornered Ana into telling him, Jorja wondered what else she'd told him, and when?

"And you know this how?"

"I told you, Jorja, I know things about you, and the way I see it, you should take me up on my offer."

She wanted to, needed to, was desperate to take his offer. "You can't help me any more than I can help you."

"You're wrong about that. I'll help you execute the heist and take care of getting it safely out of the country. I have a lot of *influence*, as you put it. I don't know the extent of the trouble you and your husband are in, but—"

"He's not my husband, he's just a friend." Her voice carried a bit more aggression than she'd intended and she instantly regretted falling for his tricks again.

Pascale didn't respond. Instead, his beguiling smile fell

upon his face once more as he waited for her to explain. Something in his eyes made her want to confess everything, share her deepest and darkest past, but she fought back.

"My friend will die if I don't get the painting. I'm sorry you will have to disappoint your wife, but I believe my motivation is a tad more dire than yours."

"You didn't let me finish. I was about to say that I could help with that."

"How, by killing the guy who's blackmailing me? No, thank you. I won't be part of a plan to murder anyone."

"Who said anything about killing the guy? Torture works just as well."

He was teasing again, she hoped.

"Either way, I can't risk it. I won't."

UP TO THIS MOMENT, Pascale thought he had hooked her, but persuading her to team up with him, proved to be much harder than he'd anticipated. And he needed to win her over. He needed her help. Without her, his plan will never work and all he'd sacrificed to get this far would be fruitless. It went against everything he stood for, or at least, once stood for. Before he needed to become someone else. This was his only chance and, as much as he didn't want to, he'd need to do whatever needed to be done.

"I AM TRULY sorry to hear that. I had hoped we could be allies. I like you, but now you leave me no choice. May the best man win, Miss Rose."

He pushed the overhead button to call the flight attendant.

Jorja's heart pounded hard against her chest. She hadn't expected him to turn on her so quickly, thought she'd have time to come up with a way to get her belt bag off the plane again. If he made good on his threat and told the captain who she was and what she was planning, it would all be over before it even started.

She watched as the attendant came closer.

"Last chance," he whispered.

"Why are you doing this?" Jorja's voice was pleading. But it was too late.

The air hostess leaned in. "You rang, Monsieur Lupin?"

Pascale's eyes bore deep into Jorja's soul, giving her one last opportunity to unite with him.

But no words escaped her and she hesitated to respond. Desperate to agree to his deal, her heart pounding in her chest, she watched in horror as he turned to speak to the attendant.

"I was wondering if I could—"

"Stop! You win, I'll do it." Jorja yelled out, feeling as if she had just betrayed all she had ever stood for. Forced into a corner, evil had once more found victory over her and left behind a dull aching in her heart.

Her rapid change of mind evoked a victorious expression in Pascale's eyes before he turned to speak to the attendant again.

"Bring me a bottle of your finest champagne, please? I believe we have something to celebrate."

CHAPTER TWENTY-FOUR

For the remainder of the flight, Jorja found herself surprisingly captivated by Pascale Lupin's knowledge of fine art. And the more he shared, the quicker her defenses dissolved. His enthusiasm toward art was eminent and, though she tried her utmost to keep him at a distance, she found herself liking him more with every passing minute. When she did allow herself to forget about the past and what lay ahead, she lost herself in their discussions over their mutual passion for the same artists. She found him intriguing, pleasant, and far too appealing, and there were one too many times she caught herself wondering if he had similar conversations with his wife and what their marriage must be like. Knowing she tread far too close to crossing her personal lines of morals and beliefs, she quickly dismissed the sinful thoughts, instead reminding herself of who he really was.

. . .

BY THE TIME they landed in Abu Dhabi, her suspicions about him proved true when his so-called influence resulted in them being privately escorted off the aircraft, passing through the security checkpoint without once being stopped or inspected.

Questions burned anew in her mind and, try as she might, he remained an enigma—something she would need to accept, for now.

A MILITARY GREEN utility vehicle stood waiting for them on the other side of the security checkpoint, and once again, she thought it didn't match the person she'd come to know on the plane—or at least what she imagined a member of an organized crime syndicate would be accustomed to. But, as she had come to already discover, Pascale Lupin was a man who was full of surprises. So far, she had seen at least three sides to him, none of which paired up, and Jorja couldn't help but remind herself that it was best to remain cautious of him.

Sitting next to him as he drove the car through the city, she could sense that he had withdrawn too. And though he had stripped off his designer jacket and rolled up the crisp white sleeves of his shirt, there was nothing casual about his demeanor. The deep furrows in his brow told her his mind was elsewhere occupied and an icy blanket of fear engulfed her insides. She knew nothing about this man, yet she chose to trust him by putting everything on the line for a painting he was essentially competing for.

She kept her eyes pinned on the road ahead, fighting the urge to ask him what he was so deep in thought over. Her curiosity piqued further when it seemed that he knew exactly where he was going, as if he had been there several times before. And once they reached the city, she could no longer restrain herself from speaking.

"Where are we going?" She asked.

His brow relaxed as he turned to answer her with the playful smile she had now come to find synonymous with the lighter side of his personality.

"If I tell you, I'd have to kill you."

He might have been smiling as he said it, but something in his voice told her he was dead serious. And when he didn't expand on his answer, she knew instinctively not to push the issue either.

When she unintentionally fiddled with her belt bag again, his eyes darting between the road and the rearview mirror, she was once again surprised by how observant he was when he spoke.

"I am a lot of things, Jorja, but I am not a killer. You can sit back and relax. You won't need your gun, at least not with me."

"I'm not worried," she lied, shocked that he had picked up on her anxiety so quickly.

"We're almost there."

"Where?" The question rolled off her tongue before she could stop it.

"Headquarters."

She shot him a sideward glance.

"Don't look so surprised. We're going to need a place to strategize, don't we?"

"Yes, of course. I just meant, well, it just sounded so official."

"Do you call it something else? You're the pro so I'm happy to take your lead on this."

"Headquarters is fine."

"Then it's settled. The team should be there already."

"Team? We never agreed—"

"Either you are extremely confident in your abilities, which I yet have to be amazed by, or you are arrogant."

She chose not to respond as anger—or embarrassment—washed into her face.

Noticing her reaction, Pascale drew his lower lip between his teeth, instantly regretting his directness.

"Sorry, subtlety isn't my strongest trait. I am sure you are quite capable of pulling off this job on your own, *if* we had more time, but given the circumstances, we need all the manpower we can get. I've known these guys for years and I trust them."

She wanted to query why he assumed she should trust them too if she didn't even know if she could trust him yet, but refrained. She would instead make sure she remained alert at all times, and that would include keeping her guard up around him.

———

HEADQUARTERS WAS a high-rise in the center of the city dwarfed by the shadow of an ultra-modern skyscraper next to it. As they neared the underground parking access, Pascale reached across to the glove compartment.

"Here, put this on."

He handed her a black headscarf.

"These guys can be a bit touchy about this sort of thing. Besides, we don't want to attract any unnecessary attention."

She hadn't even thought of covering her head—as was customary for women in the Emirates—and once again she was taken aback by his foresight.

"The British Embassy is that way, down the street. Just in case anything happens or goes wrong."

The cautionary information instantly brought about a fresh wave of nerves, made worse when the security guards stopped them at the parking entrance. She tried not to look nervous, but when her leg bounced anxiously against the glove box, her unease was obvious.

"Relax, it's just a routine check," Pascale said before he rolled down his window and spoke to the security official in fluent Arabic.

His strong French accent had her not doubt his nationality once, but suddenly she couldn't help be even more suspicious of him, especially when the security official's face lit up the instant he saw him. Now, convinced more than ever that Pascale had undoubtedly been there before, Jorja was left with even more questions. She had foolishly fallen for his charm, but alarm bells suddenly rang loud and clear in her head. Getting the job done was all that mattered and if it meant using him and his self-appointed team, she'd do whatever it took to free Ben and get her life back.

Resolute in not letting her guard down again, she followed him into the building to where they took an elevator to the top floor.

"Something the matter?" He asked when she hadn't said a word since they parked the car.

She shook her head.

"Could've fooled me. If I didn't know better, I'd think you've suddenly gone cold on me."

"I'm fine."

The elevator doors opened to a spacious but sparsely furnished office apartment combo. As they entered, a slim, striking woman stylishly dressed in black pants and a bright red blouse popped into view and greeted him with a warm smile and an even warmer embrace.

She spoke French, batting her long eyelashes and pouting her bright red lips. It was clear the two were more than just colleagues—she was his mistress—and Jorja instantly felt even more foolish for allowing herself to enjoy his earlier charms. Not to mention that it was entirely repulsive to watch since the man was already married.

"This is Jorja. Jorja, meet the heart of our team, Veronique."

Jorja felt the sick build up when Pascale turned on his charms with Veronique too, but the effervescent woman quickly pushed him aside and hooked her slender arms into Jorja's.

"I prefer Nikki. Come, let me introduce you to the others."

Dragged by the arm across the room, Jorja soon found three more members of his team scattered throughout the open plan space.

"Put that down, boys, the boss is in town and we have company." Nikki's voice grew unexpectedly stern as she chased two of the guys off the couch where they were engrossed in a Playstation game.

"Boys will be boys," she winked sideways at Jorja as she ushered her to the large glass table that stood in the center of the room. "Come on, we're on the clock now," she continued, suddenly sounding more like their mother than an associate.

Pascale smiled to himself where he poured a coffee from the machine before gesturing if Jorja wanted one too.

She nodded, feeling every bit the imposter among their obviously close-knit unit.

"You can lose the headscarf now," Pascale whispered next to her when he popped a mug of coffee in her hand.

"Of course, thanks," she said as she took the coffee and sat down at the table.

In perfect obedience to Nikki's authoritative manner, the team promptly gathered around the table, each greeting Pascale as if they were old friends.

"Everyone, meet Jorja Rose, aka Georgina Rose," Pascale announced.

Shockwaves ripped through Jorja's body at the mention of her real name. With it sprung forth an awed roar of excitement between the three men at the table. As far as the world knew, Georgina Rose died twenty years ago, so how did he know who she really was? How did any of them know?

She sat in shocked silence, desperate to piece it all together while his team's reaction left her all the more frazzled.

"No way!" the youngest of the three cheered. "I can't believe it! Boss, you said we'd be in for a treat but this? *The* Georgina Rose, right here at our table! Are you kidding us? She single-handedly brought down the entire Züber enterprise. Respect, Miss Rose." He pushed his chair back and bent at the waist as he tipped an imaginary hat toward her.

The expression on Pascale's face was that of pride as if he had just accomplished the impossible. He leaned back in his chair, enjoying the reverent display among his team as if he'd just given them an early Christmas gift. But, as hard as he tried to avoid Jorja's stern eyes that now bore holes through his head, he couldn't.

"Okay, settle down boys," he eventually said before turning to face her. "What can I say, Jorja? You're somewhat of a legend around here." He turned his focus to his team, the look on his face now serious.

"Let's leave the celebrations until after we've completed our mission, team. I'm sure Jorja will be more than willing to impart her wisdom upon us. It's going to be a long night, so let's get the formalities out of the way so we can get to work."

CHAPTER TWENTY-FIVE

But, moving on to business was not that easy for Jorja, and she stormed off in search of solitude instead. Quick to pick up on her reaction, Nikki scooted after her with Pascale close behind.

"Oh, don't pay any attention to them, Jorja. They're kids trapped in adult bodies. Just ignore them."

"I've got this, Nikki, thanks," Pascale gently cut in, and ushered Jorja into an adjacent room where he shut the door behind them. With her blood already at boiling point, Jorja didn't waste another moment before she hissed at him.

"What was that, huh? I'm not here for you and your team's amusement like I'm some kind of crazy circus animal!"

"You're right. I can only apologize. The boys were blindsided and aren't used to being in the presence of notorious professionals like you. But it came from a place of admiration. Nothing else. They are good people and they're the best at what they do. When this is all over you never have to see any of us again. Unless of course, you want to." His eyes turned playful again.

But this time, she ignored the fluttering sensations it brought about and instead turned and looked him dead in the eye.

"Who are you really, huh? What's all this? How do you know so much about me?" Suddenly she couldn't stop all the questions that still scrambled her head. She didn't trust him or any of what was happening around her. But she was trapped, forced to let him help her so she could free Ben.

"You know who I am, Jorja, and I told you, we both want the same thing. I want the painting back where it belongs in Gabrielle's family, and you need it to free Ben. I gave you my word. I'll help you when the time comes to free your friend if, in exchange, you help me return the painting."

"We both need the painting, Pascale, so this arrangement can't possibly work. Especially if you're planning to kill someone over it. In which case, I want even less to do with this. I'm leaving. Let the best man, or *wo*man win."

She spun around to leave but he grabbed hold of her arm and held her back, taking her eyes captive with his.

"I already have it all worked out, Jorja, and it won't involve anyone getting killed, I assure you. We will both get what we want. You have my word. Trust me. This job is too big for you to handle on your own and you know it."

Emotions raged inside her but, as much as she didn't want to admit it, he was right. This was a job she couldn't risk failing at, and the sooner they got it done, the sooner she'd have Ben and her life back. Who cared who he was or what he knew—or how she came alive when he as much as looked at her. He's a player, and a crooked one at that, and she would never see him again once the heist was over. Still, she needed to protect herself. She needed to stay in control, and if it meant placing her trust in him, she'd have no option but to do so.

"Let me make it clear, Pascale. I'll play ball, and when it comes to carrying out the heist, your team had better be on point. I have the final say, or I walk and you can cross swords with me to get your hands on the painting. And when this is all done, the file is sealed and we never see each other again. Understood?"

"Deal," he said far too quickly for her liking, as if he knew something she didn't.

BY THE TIME they got back to the meeting, the team had settled down and, what could have only been Nikki's doing, individually rendered their apologies. A nod from Pascale sent Nikki a signal that he had diffused the situation and that they were back in business. He cued for her to take over the rest of the briefing, to which she promptly responded.

"Right, let's move on and formally introduce you to the team, shall we? Kalihm is our guy on the ground. Born and raised here, he knows every building, back alley, supply chain, resident, and their grandmother back to front. Whatever you need, he'll deliver. It goes without saying that he is also in charge of our getaway. This here is Harry. It's not his real name, but as you might have spotted already, he looks a lot like a certain royal prince from your neck of the woods. At only twenty-two, he is also the youngest on our team. But don't let that deceive you. He minds our cyber intelligence hub and there's not a computer system anywhere in the world this guy can't hack. He's a genius when it comes to security and all things tech. And last, but not least, we have Mo. Ex U.S. Special Forces, he is obsessed with demolition and anything that causes a disruption...or distraction, as he might like to justify it. Don't let his harsh exterior and tattoos scare you, though. He's a teddy bear on the inside." She winked at him with the same flirtatious manner used on Pascale earlier which had him instantly blush with embarrassment.

"And what would your area of expertise be?" Jorja asked her.

"Aside from keeping these boys in check, I am your eyes and ears. Your wingman, if you need one. Basically, anywhere you might need an extra pair of hands."

Pascale noticed the doubt that had settled in Jorja's eyes. "Nikki's expertise comes from her love for jewelry." Pascale said, his eyes smiling at her. "Ever heard of the Millennium Dome Raid?"

"Of course."

"Well, Veronique here, was the notorious thief who very nearly got away with the Millennium Star. Estimated at the time to have been worth upward of two-hundred-and-five million pounds, it remains the most famous jewelry heist of all time. And, she would have gotten away with it too had it not been for the imbecile she recruited as getaway who had the police on his tail for car theft."

"Something you won't ever let me forget. Thank you for the reminder, which is precisely why I now take extra care who I put behind the wheel of the getaway car. It was a lesson that almost cost me everything."

They shared a suspicious silent exchange.

Pascale was quick to deflect attention away from them. "Yes, and that's why our team is the best. We get the job done. Everytime."

Jorja, who'd been silently observing the team, was both impressed and somewhat set at ease with the information she now learned.

"We have forty-eight-hours to get the painting back to Geneva," Nikki reminded quickly. "The clock is ticking."

"Then let's do this," Jorja said.

"Excellent, so, now that we're all on the same page and

playing nicely, I believe you have the secret ingredient to getting this party started." Nikki looked at Jorja.

"Yes, of course."

THOUGH STILL NOT FULLY CONVINCED THAT she could truly trust them or that they were on the same side, Jorja reached across to the notepad and pen that lay in the middle of the table. As she wrote down the address she had stolen from Franz's files, she silently pleaded with God that Pascale and his team were being truthful and that she wasn't making a colossal mistake by teaming up with them.

But, come what may, she knew she was ready and she passed the details to Nikki, her hands trembling as she did so. There was no stopping it now. All she could do was trust God and execute the best robbery she had ever pulled. And as she watched the team scatter into action, she found Pascale's warm eyes suddenly upon her. What she saw behind them was nothing she'd expected or seen before. Instead, she saw a deep sense of gratitude, as if what she was doing, meant more to him than life itself. Perhaps it was motivated by the love for his wife, or something else her instincts had not yet fully revealed to her.

Or perhaps she was imagining that he needed her because she'd finally gotten the chance to do again what she'd been yearning for since she first went into hiding all those years ago.

But, as guilt-ridden as she was over being forced into

wrongdoing, whatever it was had unexpectedly lit her up on the inside and made her flash a small smile in reply.

THE NIGHT DREW ON AND, for the most part, the team worked in perfect silence as each did their part to gather the necessary information they required to execute the heist. Pascale had suspiciously disappeared less than an hour after they started, leaving Jorja on edge all over again. He had said he needed to meet up with someone and it was as if his team found nothing untoward about it. But when she asked Nikki who he was meeting, she clammed up like a shell, playing it off as if it was nothing out of the ordinary for Pascale to do whenever he was in town.

"Don't you think he should be here with us, though?" Jorja had asked, to which Nikki shrugged her shoulders, pouted her red lips, and confidently assured her that he was probably just catching up with an old friend.

"Have you known each other long?" Jorja had asked her again where they pored over fresh information Kalihm had gathered.

"Long enough. Now, let's get to work on these blueprints, shall we?" She turned her attention to Harry.

"Anything on the security system yet?"

"Nada, and by the looks of it, we might need to get inside for a full recon to know what we're up against."

"Can you work your magic with a way in?"

Kalihm answered instead. "The man has a thing for

baguettes. So much so that he insists a daily fresh batch gets delivered all the way from a bakery in Dubai."

"I can intercept the delivery van," Mo volunteered.

"No explosives, Mo. We don't need to draw any attention to us before we've even started. Besides, we're going to need the van, and be gentle with the delivery guy," she warned.

Mo gestured a salute in response, after which he got up and started scratching around in a black duffle bag he had on a table in the far corner.

"I'll get onto the clothes. I can almost guarantee the driver has to wear an overall or an apron or something." Kalihm jumped in and moved toward the door.

"You up for a delivery, Jorja?" Nikki smiled.

"Sounds good."

"What does?" Pascale suddenly said behind them.

"Delivering fresh baguettes," Harry sneered. "Our target is obsessed with them."

"Interesting," Pascale said as he set down a batch of fresh coffee and *rigag*—a traditional sweetened crepe-like bread—on the table. "Tell me what you know while it's hot."

CHAPTER TWENTY-SIX

Nikki was quick to respond with an update of their preliminary reconnaissance. "The address Jorja gave us traces to Sheikh Zuhalil Bin Nasr, loosely translated to Saturn Eagle. He has three wives and five daughters, one of whom, the eldest, is engaged to a Dubai prince. A fourth-generation oil magnate who made most of his new money in cars and real estate, he's quite the big spender. By the looks of things, our eagle enjoys everything to the extreme. Which brings us to the real juicy stuff: his not-so-humble abode. It's located on the edge of the city and backs up to the desert. From our initial external imagery, it looks to be somewhat of a fortress."

"Security?" Pascale asked.

"Unconfirmed at this stage, Boss," Harry shouted from behind his three large computer monitors. "His security system is military grade. I can't access it externally."

"We're working on getting inside," Nikki continued.

"The baguette delivery," Pascale stated.

"Exactly. There's a daily delivery. With Mo's help, we'll intercept the truck."

"And it will work?" Pascale queried.

"Yep, we're good," Harry yelled out. "I just hacked the baker's system. Our next delivery is scheduled at five a.m. I've already copied the designated driver's identification pass from his mobile and transferred it to this one. It's a simple QR code and it is ready to go." He slid a mobile device into one corner of his desk.

"I'll drive, you hide in the back. Once we get through the gates, I'll distract and delay while you sneak in," Nikki said to Jorja, to which she nodded in agreement.

"They'll be able to gain access into the property via the service entrance, which takes them to the kitchen at the rear of the house. From there, they're on their own. As soon as Jorja locks into the wifi address, it will ping back to me. Once I have that, I'll be able to hack into their servers, surveillance, and anything else that will tell us where he's keeping the painting."

"Good job, everyone. We have a little over two hours until the delivery so let's get it going," Pascale announced.

BUT, shortly after the team had made their final preparations to execute the infiltration, Kalihm burst through the door in full theatrical display.

"Houston, we have a problem. The baguette delivery is a no-go. I repeat, the baguette delivery—"

"Yes, okay, we get it, Buzz Lightyear. Get on with it," Mo said, annoyed.

"You're such a party pooper," Kalihm said before he continued. "As I said, the delivery is a big fat negative. Word on the ground is the target called it off due to the wedding."

"What wedding?" Nikki asked.

"His daughter's getting married to the prince later today and, apparently, he's throwing the biggest feast the Emirates has ever seen tonight. Rumor has it that he invited around five hundred guests."

"Great, there goes that," Mo groaned.

"Not necessarily," Jorja said.

"We're listening?" Pascale prompted.

"It's the perfect opportunity to steal the painting."

"You want to pull this job today? Impossible. We're not ready," Nikki said as her hands settled onto her hips.

"I know, but hear me out. Everyone is there for the wedding, right? No one is going to be expecting a burglary. It's the perfect distraction. Even if he had a full security team at every entrance, watching so many guests is going to be a challenge, even for the best of them. I say we do it at the wedding. It might be our only chance," Jorja announced.

The room fell silent and she watched as the team looked to Pascale for feedback.

"Don't look at me. She knows what she's talking about. I trust her."

Nikki cocked her head at Pascale, frowning with disbelief at his bold statement. "There is no way we can carry out a recon and prep in under twelve hours. It's too risky."

Again, Pascale looked to Jorja. "You sure about this, Jorja?"

Jorja wasn't. In truth, her stomach was tied in knots and anxiety grew in her chest, but she had no intentions of letting them know.

"If there is one thing I've learned in this job, it is to be ready to improvise. Nothing ever goes as planned in any event, so I'm confident with the cumulative experience we all have, we can do it." She turned to face Kalihm. "We're going to need sufficient transport that will get us through the desert, fast. The way I see it, it's our best getaway route. With that many guests, the entrance to the property will be congested with cars. We'll do it Prince of Persia style, over the south wall."

Mo was quick to respond. "I can detonate a distraction remotely, to lure security's attention to the north side of the property, the exit is to the West, which means they will all make their way out the front. I'll make sure we have ropes ready."

"The walls are too high to climb," Harry said.

"Then I'll use the tactical grappling launchers. It's silent, shoots a distance of one-hundred-and-fifteen feet, and I'll have it ready by the time you make it to the wall. Consider it done," Mo assured them.

"That will work. Kalihm, can you be ready on the other side with our getaway transport?" Jorja asked.

"Your wish is my command. Leave it to me."

"Hello? Have you guys lost your minds? It's all dandy that you've got our getaway route planned, but have you stopped to consider how we're meant to pull off the actual job first? We don't know anything about the security system or, most importantly, where he's keeping the painting. Not to mention how we're planning on getting away with hundreds of people attending his daughter's wedding! This is suicide. It will never work. We need more time."

"We don't have any more time, Nikki," Pascale said.

"Why, because she has a deadline? We don't, so I fail to understand why we're risking our lives for her."

Her outburst instantly turned Pascale's eyes dark with warning.

"She knows?" Jorja queried. "I can't believe you told her. You were the one who asked for my help, remember? I told you, I can do this on my own."

"Knows what?" Mo asked on behalf of the rest of the team who now looked equally suspicious.

"Sorry, I shouldn't have said anything. Forget it, we'll

figure something out." Nikki quickly tried to remedy her mistake.

"If there's something that puts us all at risk then we have the right to know," Mo challenged. "We're trusting you as much as you are trusting us, Jorja," he continued.

"You can trust me," Pascale said, his voice as assertive as his sudden commanding presence. "We're doing it tonight. Last I checked, you were the best at what we do, so stay focused and let's get it done. Harry, speak to me."

"Copy that, Boss. Getting Jorja on the guest list is the easy part. She'll need a male plus one, of course, and no offense, Mo, but your facial tats won't pass you as a distinguished guest." He raised one ginger eyebrow in Pascale's direction.

"No problem. What else?" Pascale agreed to the obscured suggestion that was cast his way.

"I've installed the grabber on your phone. They will no doubt deploy extra protocols in their security to monitor mobile activity, so we will have a very small window to grab the wifi network address before they lock your phone from their IP sequence. I would need you to activate the app the moment you step through the entrance. You're going to need to hover in the same spot as close to the threshold as possible. I'd say about ten seconds, before your mobile's signal switches over to theirs. Once I'm in, we'll have to move quickly. Unfortunately, since I won't have any time to recon their system and test their capabilities, I don't know what we're up against yet and literally anything can go wrong at any point. Improvisation and quick thinking will be vital. I'll have to work quickly from there, figuring it out as we go along."

"Let's prepare for every eventuality and pull all tech we have access to," Pascale instructed as he looked over Jorja's shoulder where she was studying the blueprints. "Any guesses?" he said, referring to where the painting might be hidden.

"It could be anywhere, really, but I recall Ana saying Jürgen had mentioned that it was behind a wall. The actual painting is only twenty-six by seventeen-and-a-half inches in size, but it would be foolish to assume that it's the only item he has hidden. In my experience, someone who has held onto an item of this value for this amount of time will no doubt have stocked up on other items that carry less collateral value."

"Holding back his trump card then," Nikki spoke again for the first time.

"Precisely."

"So, we just won't know until we're inside to assess where security is the tightest," Nikki stated, looking concerned.

Pascale's eyes narrowed where he'd been watching Jorja work. He had seen something in her behavior that piqued his curiosity.

"You already know where it is, don't you?"

"I might, but it's a long shot, and I could be entirely wrong. But if it were me, I'd keep something as valuable an asset as the *Salvator Mundi* separate from my less valuable inventory. Also, he must have dozens of staff on his property, so getting these items in and out of his property unnoticed would require separate access to the usual entry points."

"There were reports several years ago that he had used an external German construction company to modify the stables at his home. It was rumored that he spent over a million dollars for two weeks' work, which, frankly, we all frowned over. Yes, the man has an impressive stud of racehorses, but I remember thinking at the time that he was insane to spend more than triple the amount needed to upgrade his already adequate equestrian facilities." Kalihm conveyed.

"That does sound fishy," Pascale agreed.

"His stables are situated on the eastern side of the property, but these blueprints don't extend to his equestrian facilities," Jorja reported.

"Already on it," Harry affirmed from behind his screen where his fingers clanked the keys. "Got it! Kalihm is right. Looks like it was a huge, covert construction project. These are the blueprints before the construction. I'm still working on tracking the company he used, but it looks like they made sure there weren't any trails left behind." He sent the blueprints to the overhead computer screen on the nearby wall.

"So, are we saying he's got the painting somewhere in

his stables? That changes everything," Nikki said, now looking to Jorja for answers.

But Jorja was too busy studying the blueprints to comment, her attention darting between the two sets of blueprints. As if they each already knew her enough to realize that her genius mind was finding a way around the issue, they left her alone, watching her every movement. And when, merely ten minutes later, a smile broke on Jorja's face, the team instantly knew she had cracked the mystery.

CHAPTER TWENTY-SEVEN

All eyes were on Jorja as they waited with bated breaths to hear what she had just uncovered. And when she finally spoke, the team was visibly on edge.

"He's keeping the painting here," Jorja announced, pointing to a spot on the main property's blueprints.

Her bold statement left the room stunned with silence, their eyes questioningly searching each other to make sure they'd understood her correctly. It was Pascale who spoke on behalf of his team.

"You're sure? The kitchen and not the stables?"

Jorja nodded. "I'm very certain."

Nikki mumbled obscenities in French before she went at it with Jorja. "And what exactly makes you so sure it's there? We just heard the man spent a fortune on construction in a place that would make perfect sense to hide his antiquities, and now you're telling us it's in his kitchen, the single most occupied space in his entire property? Sorry, Pascale, I mean no insult, but this is ridiculous. You're pinning all your trust on what she says. She's going to cost us everything!"

Pascale looked nervous too. Caught between Nikki and Jorja, two of the world's most experienced antiquity thieves, Pascale struggled to unravel it all. Nothing Jorja said made any sense to him and, in contrast, everything Nikki had said, he agreed, sounded entirely logical. But his gut pulled him toward believing the implausible instead and he waited for Jorja to prove his instincts right.

"You're absolutely correct, Nikki," Jorja finally said, throwing her hands in the air as she shrugged. "It's insane. It makes no sense to hide something worth nearly half a million dollars where they prepare food all day long. The place is practically crawling with teams of insignificant people."

Nikki noted the sarcasm in her voice and grunted, casting a look of warning her way.

"Let her speak, Nikki," Pascale told her, which infuriated her even more.

Jorja stood up and walked over to the equestrian center's blueprints on the large screen.

"See this?" She circled a spot on the screen with her finger, then continued. "This is where he has the main treasury. Transported in and out with his horse trailers, no one suspects anything because it's a known fact that thoroughbred racehorses warrant top security and constant surveillance. His horses are worth a small fortune entirely on their own, and it makes absolute sense to keep them under high security conditions."

"So what, that doesn't mean the painting's not there," Nikki spat again.

"No, but you and I both know that in our line of business, a ruse is your target's best defense. As Sherlock Holmes once said, 'nothing is more deceptive than the obvious fact'."

Nikki fell silent as she suddenly realized precisely what Jorja was saying. She smiled and shook her head, then dropped it back and laughed toward the heavens.

"You're right, Pascale, she is the best. I owe you an apology, Jorja. I don't know how I didn't see it."

"Okay, can someone please tell me what's going on here?" Kalihm said, looking as confused as the rest.

"He hid it in the last place anyone would ever think to look for it," Pascale smiled, pride over Jorja's accomplishment—or perhaps because it meant he was one step closer to finally getting what he had been working for—clearly written all over his face.

"It's actually quite genius," Nikki said, still in awe of Jorja's brilliance.

"Wait, let me get this straight. The eagle hid a piece of fine art, worth half a million dollars, one that has been missing for years, somewhere inside his kitchen? No security, no subterranean vault, simply in plain sight? Well, that's going to be the most boring job yet," Mo said, looking annoyed that his tactical skills won't be needed.

"Oh, calm down, Rambo. I'll let you blow up ten cars when this is all said and done, okay?" Nikki mocked.

"Actually, I wouldn't discount the level of complexity," Jorja countered. "It doesn't mean he won't have it under tight security measures, it just means that it won't necessarily attract the same amount of attention his main vault does. In other words, security might not be as obvious. My guess is he'd have minor security detail on it, but will then have several complex security obstacles to overcome."

"The place could be booby trapped too," Mo said.

"Most likely, yes," Jorja agreed.

"I'm sending both of you in," Pascale announced to Jorja and Nikki. "You each bring a different skillset to the table. Can't hurt to be prepared."

"Fine by me," Jorja said, smiling at Nikki who was visibly caught off guard with how easily Jorja put their earlier spat behind her.

"I'll be honored to work alongside you, Jorja." she extended her own olive branch.

Pascale turned their attention back to the schematics.

"Any suggestions where the safe might be?"

"It could be anywhere but my guess is it's somewhere in this vicinity. There are several rooms leading off the kitchen. None of which leads back into the main house or has an exit. My guess is it might be used for food storage, table linens, that sort of thing," Jorja ventured.

"We won't know for sure until we're inside though," Nikki said as she looked to Harry.

"Already on it," Harry announced, then continued to report as his fingers worked the computer keys. "It's too late to have you join the main staff roll, so I'm adding you to the catering staff list instead. They're using a private company to cater the entire event. That's our only way into the kitchen at such short notice."

"Send me the company's details and I'll have the uniforms ready to go in an hour," Kalihm requested, his phone buzzing with the information moments later.

"What else?" Pascale prompted Harry who was back at it on his computer.

"And, if I'm right, and I think I am, the kitchen and main house will run on their own separate server that won't extend to the main vault's security in the equestrian center. Minimizing vulnerabilities with the center's distance from the main house would be the primary reason for this. It most likely runs off a secondary server—"

"You're getting distracted, Harry. Cut to the chase." Nikki brought him back to the task.

"The bottom line is, I'm still going to need someone to grab the sequence from the main house so I can access the mainframe and infiltrate the security system. The kitchen wifi might have been isolated to protect the security of the main server." Harry's fingers ran over the keys, hitting the final key that secured their access. "And we're done. Tags are printing as we speak."

"Keep me on the guest list," Pascale said. "I'll grab the sequence as per our previous plan."

"We're going to need you too, Mo," Jorja said. "I'm not entirely sure how and where yet, but once we're inside, I'll let you know. Be on standby...here." She pointed to a spot on the map.

"Copy that."

"There's just one problem," Nikki suddenly announced as she stood looking over the blueprints again. "The kitchen doesn't back onto the desert anymore. If we wanted to plan our escape through the desert, we'd need to make our way around the front, across the courtyard, and past the main foyer. How do we get past all those people without being seen?"

"Leave that to me," Mo said, sporting a grin so wide they thought his face was going to crack.

"Well, then, let's get suited up and prepped, team. We need to be sharp and ready for every eventuality. All hands on deck and leave no room for error. And, Harry, make sure the comms are up. Communication is going to be key. Kalihm, please go ahead with your initial getaway through the desert. Any problems, let us know. Mo, set up the grappling launchers and be ready for extraction over this wall, here." Pascale pointed to a spot on the property as he set out instructions to his team. When he was done, and his team was engrossed in their preparations, he stepped away to the far corner of the room where he took out his phone to make a call.

From where Jorja sat at the table, finalizing details with Nikki, who in turn handed their list of required items to Kalihm, Jorja couldn't hear who Pascale was talking to. He had turned his back toward them and spoke in subdued tones. But even as doubt crossed her mind again, she concluded that the call was most likely to his wife and she tore her heedful gaze away from him to focus instead on the heist.

WITH ALL POSSIBLE contingencies predicted and primed, the team took up their positions as strategized. As the VIP guests arrived for the wedding reception, so did their security entourage, which instantly increased the team's anxiety. Pascale lingered outside the main entrance, reporting his findings over their in-ear communication apparatus.

"We're good, keep it cool," he instructed.

On the other end of the estate, Jorja and Nikki had just entered the kitchen via the service entrance, disguised as catering staff.

"You must be the newbies. You're late! These platters aren't going to fill themselves. Get on it, and make sure your hands are washed!" the catering supervisor said as he caught sight of them.

"Won't happen again," Jorja replied as they fell in with the other staff in the kitchen.

"We're in," she reported over the comms to the team as soon as it was safe.

"Copy that. Harry, get ready, I'm next in line," Pascale informed from where he now stood waiting to pass through the access-controlled entrance.

"Ready, Boss. Standing by."

CHAPTER TWENTY-EIGHT

W hen it came to his turn, Pascale stepped up to the pleasant host at the door who was flanked by two armed guards on either side of the large double-door entrance.

"Welcome, sir, can I have your invitation please?"

Pascale patted down the pockets of his tuxedo. "I have it here somewhere. Hang on a second," he stalled, imitating an absentminded trait.

"Hold it, Boss, I need a few more seconds," Harry reported in his ear, to which Pascale responded with more theatrics to delay his access.

"Forgive me, I was certain I put it in my jacket pocket. This is why you need a wife, right?" Pascale made small talk.

"Sir, I'm going to need to ask you to please step aside

until you find your invitation so we don't hold up the evening's events."

"I definitely have it in one of my pockets. If you can just give me a few more moments. I had it just a few minutes ago." Pascale continued to pat down his pockets, pretending to search for his invitation.

"Sir, step aside, please?" one of the security men instructed Pascale.

Pascale—and Harry—felt every bit of pressure that now escalated as they raced against the time needed to break into the security server.

"Almost there, Boss, two more seconds, wait ... got it!" Harry yelled in his ear.

Relieved, Pascale produced his invitation in the nick of time, leaving the host and his security men puffing with annoyance as they allowed him into the house.

"Good job, Harry. Talk about shaving it thin," Pascale said once he stepped inside. "How long before you crack the server?"

"Not sure, Boss, but I'm working as fast as I can."

"Standing by," Pascale said, after which Jorja and Nikki echoed the same.

A SHORT WHILE later Harry reported to the team. "Guys, we're facing a beast. This might not be as easy as we had hoped."

"Talk to us, Harry," Jorja said.

"Well, let's just say this guy's security system is state of the art. I mean, for a start, I can only be in their system for fifteen seconds at a time before they detect me. If I had time beforehand, I could've cracked the bypass, but, without the password, there's no way around it."

"What does that mean, Harry?" Pascale asked.

"It means that I have to exit, wait ten seconds, then loop back in, fifteen seconds at a time."

"So anything can happen during the ten seconds you're offline," Pascale stated.

"Yup, but that's not all, boss. He has surveillance cameras all over the place with live feeds to the security hub in the west wing of the house, and that's only the beginning."

"Then let's start there and take it as we go. Can you replace the live feed surveillance cameras and bypass it with static shots?" Nikki suggested.

"I should be able to, yes. I won't have time to run a long enough video feed with only fifteen seconds in the system, but I can take some static images and loop them."

"What about the painting? Have you located it yet?" Jorja asked, now eager to get started.

"There's a bigger cluster of security cameras leading up towards a room to your right. Heat maps are picking up motion sensors in one of the walls so I'm pretty sure that's where it is."

"Direct us," Jorja said as she transferred more canapés onto a gold platter.

"Through the door directly behind you and turn left into the small corridor, then access the third door on your right. That opens up to a long corridor which leads into the room. There are five surveillance cameras along the way and they're all hot."

"Yes, I noticed the one above the door behind me earlier. It's pointing directly at my back. Take a static shot now and one as I turn to hand off the tray. Then, another with me out of the shot. Once you start looping, I'll need about seven seconds to pick the lock on the door. We will have to do it during the ten seconds you're locked out of the server. I'll wait until you are back in before we switch to the corridor's statics."

"Copy that, rolling now. I've already run statics on both corridors and the room so we're ready to switch when you give the go. The door to the vault room carries a digitalized double-locking system. It shouldn't be too hard to bypass, but unfortunately that's where my visual access stops. There are no surveillance cameras inside that room so, apart from the heat pads I detected in the wall earlier, I have no idea what's behind that door."

"Noted. Nikki, where are you at?" Jorja asked.

"Heading back from the foyer to fill my tray."

"I need you to create a distraction and stop anyone from coming into the kitchen while the statics are running. Something that's also long enough to give me time to open the door. I'm alone in the kitchen right now, but the next team of servers would be picking up their fresh platters any moment now."

"I can help with that," Pascale interjected. "I'll come to you, Nikki. Stay put."

The team executed the plan as agreed and it wasn't long before Pascale found Nikki. Together, they moved closer to the kitchen, where they remained in position, blocking off the entrance.

"Incoming," Nikki reported when she spotted two servers heading straight for them.

When they were upon them, Pascale clutched at his chest and tumbled to the floor. Nikki immediately joined the theatrical display and before long, a small crowd of guests had gathered around them, successfully blocking off the entry into the kitchen.

Quick to execute, Harry and Jorja set their plan into motion, and it took less than the estimated seven seconds for Jorja to pick the lock on the door in the kitchen.

"Got it," she quickly reported.

"Copy that, on my way," Nikki replied, after which Pascale tuned down his performance.

"I'm okay." Pascale continued the role-play. "Probably just indigestion."

"Let's get you some ice for that nasty bump on your head, sir." Nikki quickly improvised and helped him to his feet before she ushered him toward the kitchen.

"It's okay, everyone, he's okay. Give him some space, please? I'll take him to the kitchen while you focus on the other guests," she continued, ordering the nearby waiting staff to take the onlookers back to the reception.

"Start the loop now," Nikki instructed Harry as they met with Jorja in the kitchen.

"Copy that. Loop is live. Switching to the loop in the corridor in three...two...one, now," Harry counted down as he followed through on the hijacking sequence to ensure Nikki and Jorja gained access through the door undetected.

"We're in," Nikki reported as soon as they exited the kitchen via the unlocked door, at which time Pascale snuck out the service exit and made his way toward the lawns where a few guests had spilled over into the garden patio.

"And we're clear," Harry announced, switching the kitchen's loop off. "My window is closing in three seconds. You will have to bypass the digital lock on the door yourself, I'm afraid. You're on your own, ladies."

"Copy that," Nikki replied as they made their way to the third door on the right, as per Harry's earlier reconnaissance.

"How long will the static loop last?" Nikki asked Jorja when they reached the door.

"Hopefully long enough to give me time to bypass this lock. Here, take one."

"Gum? You're giving me gum at a time like this?"

"It will help with the nerves and you never know when you'll need it, trust me."

"I was wrong before so I won't argue." Nikki popped

the piece of gum in her mouth, now noticing that Jorja had already attached a digital code grabbing device to the door and started running it.

The numbers on the screen ticked away slowly, causing a wave of tension to ripple through her body.

"Come on, come on," Nikki spoke to the machine as she anxiously kept one eye on the overhead camera's red light that would switch back on when the loop ran out.

In silence, they watched the device scan through the various combination sequences, willing it to go faster.

"I'm back in, ladies," Harry announced.

"We're having issues with the lock, Harry. When's the loop running out?" Nikki checked.

"Not for another thirty seconds. I thought to take extra precautions."

Four more seconds ticked by.

"What's taking so long?" Nikki asked.

"I told you the security was top notch. You've got a twelve-code sequence instead of the usual five," Harry informed them.

"We're going to run out of loop, Harry. Can you loop it again?"

"Already busy with it. My window is about to close again. And I'm out."

Nikki's eyes shot up to the surveillance camera where, for the briefest of time, the single red light blinked before it went off again.

CHAPTER TWENTY-NINE

"Tell me you got the loop going before we went live," Nikki said.

"I did, but I have no idea if they spotted you in the few seconds before I switched it back. I'm still locked out of the system."

Jorja shot up a silent prayer, her stomach in knots as she once again begged God for His mercy.

"What's taking so long? They could come bursting through that door any second now," Nikki complained.

"There are literally millions of sequences to work through, it takes time."

"Precisely what we don't have."

"We're on the last number, not long now," Jorja said, her eyes pinned to the fast-changing red digits on her device.

URCELIA TEIXEIRA

A few much-too-long moments later, the lock clicked over and unbolted the door.

"Harry, we got it but it looks like there's an auto lock. We need to switch to the static loop on the other side of this door now, before the lock resets," Jorja stressed.

"A few more seconds, hang on."

Tensions ran high as time ticked by, forcing them to wait for Harry to gain access to the security system once more.

"Clear!" Harry yelled as soon as he switched the surveillance cameras over, and not a moment too soon.

Nikki squeezed through the door first, Jorja close behind her. Checking first that the red light was off on the overhead surveillance camera, Nikki charged toward the door at the end of the hallway.

"Stop!" Jorja yelled, yanking her by the arm just in time before she pushed Nikki's body against the wall, then pinned her own flush against the opposite wall.

"What are you doing?" Nikki asked, her voice laced with annoyance.

"Stick to the wall and don't move a muscle."

"What? Why?"

Jorja dropped her eyes toward the motion sensor directly next to Nikki's thighs.

"There's one on my side too."

"What's happening, ladies?" Harry asked with trepidation.

"We have motion sensors, Harry. Two of them, about

two or three feet above the floor, directly opposite each other. Any alarms go off on your end?" Jorja asked.

"Negative, security is still unaware of anything. But be careful, my time is up again soon," Harry warned.

"I don't know much about motion sensors, except that they usually have a limited field of vision." Nikki confessed.

"That's true, and they all have a blind spot," Jorja said. "And these ones are located directly below them."

"I guess they weren't expecting any toddlers to rob them," Harry joked in their ears.

"Not the time, Harry darling," Nikki scolded, feeling every bit of tension in the situation.

Jorja slowly turned her head toward her shoulder, affording her a better vantage point from which to study the devices more closely.

"Can you deactivate them, Harry?" she asked.

"Nope, they weren't visible anywhere on the server, so I am assuming they aren't connected. In other words, they are operating independently, most likely via bluetooth that's controlled manually."

"Like a remote control," Nikki simplified.

"More likely via a mobile app, but yes. Sorry ladies, nothing I can do for you on this end except to keep an eye out for anyone coming once I'm back in."

"Now what?" Nikki asked Jorja.

"Now we say a prayer and hope my home-hack works."

"Whatever that is, I reckon it is worth a try, right? What do you need me to do?"

"Slide down toward the floor, slowly, and as low as you can, go. Stay as close to the wall as possible. Not too fast, slower," Jorja instructed as Nikki made too many sudden movements.

When they were both on floor, their legs tucked beneath them and their backs flush with the walls, Jorja gave the next instruction.

"Now, slowly unclip your access card from your apron. Careful, keep it slow."

When they had both done it, Jorja smiled at Nikki.

"Still have that piece of gum I gave you? Now is the time to use it."

"I'm in awe, Miss Rose. It is no wonder I was the one who got caught. You truly are a legend."

"Yeah, well, there's always a first time. We're not out of the woods just yet."

Jorja took a deep breath before she continued, suddenly haunted by a sinking feeling in the pit of her stomach.

"We need to attach the cards over the sensors very slowly, moving in from directly below the eyes. That's where the blind spots are. The trick is that we have to do it at precisely the same time. Once the cards cover the eyes, you can stick it down to the sensor unit with your gum. It should hold until we return. Remember, we have to do it at the exact moment or they'll get triggered. And no sudden movements. Easy and smooth is the key."

"Noted. Ready when you are."

The pair worked together in perfect synchronicity, their bodies taut as they strained to maintain their awkward off-balance positions while each slowly slid their identification badges over the sensors. Neither spoke and both barely breathed, holding their hands steady until they finally completed the delicate task.

The pair remained frozen in position, anticipating an alarm to sound at any second. But nothing happened.

"Think it worked?" Nikki asked.

"I guess we will soon find out."

Crawling side by side like snakes, they slid across the floor and underneath the invisible lines that once connected the two sensors. When they reached the other side and slowly rose to their feet, they stood in place, waiting to see if they were successful.

"You're clear, ladies. The loop is still running and no alarms were detected on the system," Harry set them at ease the moment he had entered his next fifteen second window.

Roughly six yards of hallway stood between them and the door to the vault room, and Jorja slowly turned to walk toward it.

But it was Nikki's turn to showcase her expertise.

"Hold it! Not so fast. I'm afraid this is not going to be a

stroll in the park, my friend. I think we've got ourselves another booby trap."

"Yup, I see it." Jorja had already popped on her laser detection goggles.

"What, what are you seeing?" Harry asked, sounding nervous.

"A laser grid spanning the entire corridor," Nikki answered.

"Of course there's one." He dropped an expletive before he continued, his fingers clicking the keys. "Found it!"

"Talk to us, Harry," Nikki begged.

"It's heavily encrypted."

"Can you crack it?" Jorja asked.

"Yes, but not within my window, I need a whole lot more time. It's got a protection sequence built in that resets each time I leave," Harry reported. "I'll keep trying but the sequencing is too complicated."

"Standing by. Harry, work your magic," Nikki said.

But, regardless of Harry's exceptional hacking skills, time was against them, and he was soon disconnected from the system again.

"I'm out, guys. It's just too intricate to breach in such a short pocket of time."

The pair contemplated their options.

"How well can you see the lasers with your goggles?" Nikki asked.

"Clear as day. I'll be able to navigate it for sure."

"Then you go ahead. I'll wait for Harry to get back online and work his magic. We can't waste any more time."

"Guys, we have a problem! It seems there is a routine check scheduled and they're heading your way."

"How long, Harry?" Nikki checked.

"Three minutes, if we're lucky."

"That's not enough time for me to make it back or for us to get out of here," Jorja replied.

"I'll hold them off. Go finish the job, Jorja."

But Jorja wasn't one to easily give up or leave a man behind.

"If you stick close to me, the gaps are large enough to go through together. As long as you copy my movements precisely. We can do it, Nikki. I'm not leaving you behind."

"Even if we make it, we still have to find our way out of the safe room, and that's impossible because there's no exit."

"Let's cross that bridge when we get to it, okay? This can work, now, let's go!" Jorja rushed her.

With no alternative, and no time to waste, Nikki fell in directly behind Jorja, pushing her body tightly against her back.

"Ready?"

"As I'll ever be," Nikki replied.

Together they started, tackling the intricate laser grid one motion at a time, their bodies glued together like sheets of paper. When they were halfway through, Harry's voice in their ears was tense and filled with concern.

"They've just entered the kitchen. My guess is they're seconds away from entering through the door to the first hallway. They seem to be chatting up one of the girls in the kitchen. And I've just lost my vision, I'm out again."

Neither Jorja or Nikki acknowledged his warning as their full focus was pinned on navigating the intricate web of lasers. Slowly, methodically, one step at a time, one acrobatic move little by little, they continued in deafening silence.

When Harry's window opened again, his voice was near frantic.

"We're out of time, ladies! They are right outside the door!"

But Jorja and Nikki had one final step left to take. And as they did so, a loud alarm came from somewhere above their heads.

CHAPTER THIRTY

Convinced they had accidentally tripped the laser, panic ripped through their bodies. Bound by their craft and joint emotions of fear, Jorja and Nikki rushed toward the vault room.

"We're good, ladies. I just tripped the alarm at the opposite side of the house. It should buy you a little bit of time."

"Good thinking, Harry. Thank you," Nikki said, relieved.

"It's not going to last forever, though. I am sure they'll be making their way back to you soon. Did you make it through the lasers?"

"We did. We're outside the vault room," Jorja reported.

"Is it just me or are there no locks on this door?" Nikki asked, her eyes searching around the frame of the door.

"Nope, there's nothing here. Harry, any hidden traps visible on your end?" Jorja asked.

"Not that I'm able to detect, no, but remember, I have zero access to the vault room. Who knows what to expect once you walk through that door?"

"Copy that, loud and crystal clear," Nikki said with a trembling voice where she now watched Jorja inspect the door.

She had placed her cheek flush against the door as she listened for any signs of electronic mechanisms, gently gliding her hands over the door and its frame.

"What are you looking for?" Nikki eventually asked.

"I'm not sure."

"Are you thinking there's a tripwire hidden here somewhere?"

"There's always a chance. Never assume anything," she said, as her thoughts instantly went to Ben when she absentmindedly quoted his favorite teaching.

"Great, okay, well, what do you say we take a chance and go straight for the handle? Strange as the thing might be, time isn't exactly on our side."

Jorja had noticed the door handle too. It was out of place for a door of its nature since it resembled the lever handles one would ordinarily find on the door to a cold storage room.

"I agree. You're out of time," Harry echoed. "I'm back in and you're about to get company. They're coming down the corridor now."

Jorja closed her hand over the door handle, briefly shutting her eyes while she yanked back on the lever. The door hissed as air released from behind the suction pads inside the frame, revealing a pitch dark room on the other side of it.

"It's a fridge? Really?" Nikki whispered, stunned at the discovery.

"Go, go, go, they're about to walk in behind you!"

Harry's warning came just in time, giving them the slightest of moments to quickly sneak inside. Once more air sucked from the frame as the door shut and sealed behind them. Above their heads, a light switched on automatically, revealing around them a small room just large enough to fit a double bed. Its walls glowed bright white and were entirely smooth, matching the same brilliant white resin floor that ran up to the ceiling.

"Harry, we're in. What's the status of our visitors?" Nikki requested.

But no answer came back.

"Harry, can you hear me? I repeat, what's the status of the guards?"

"We've lost comms, Nikki. It's no use. These walls are four inches thick and made from high-grade steel. It's completely soundproof too."

Nikki turned around to find the door handle, but there wasn't one.

"We can't get out, Jorja, look, there's no handle."

"There has to be a way out, we just need to look for it."

URCELIA TEIXEIRA

"We're trapped inside a giant cooler box, Jorja. Look around you! There are no windows, levers, handles, nothing, and especially not a safe of any kind or the painting. You sounded so certain of yourself, insisting this was where he kept his painting. It sounded ridiculous then and it's proven to be nothing but a waste of time."

Jorja ignored her as she continued to inspect every smooth area of every wall.

"Did you hear me, Jorja? We're trapped inside with no way out, thanks to you."

"Do you always give up this easily?"

"I'm not giving up, just stating the obvious. We have no communications with HQ, and no idea if those security guards will be barging through the door with a bunch of loaded guns."

"Well, they won't, so stop fussing and help me look for the painting."

Nikki growled in frustration.

"There is no vault and no painting, Jorja. Being in hiding all these years has clearly made you lose your touch. Times have changed since you were pulling jobs."

"It's here."

"You seem very certain of yourself, so go on then, prove me wrong."

"Then tell me, Nikki, why take the time to install digital locks, motion sensors, and an intricate laser grid system outside this room if there was nothing in here to hide, huh?"

Her question had Nikki at a loss for words while she tried to rationalize her earlier claims. But, try as she might, she couldn't. Jorja had a very valid point and she instantly felt remorse for her slanderous comments.

"You're right, I'm sorry, again. I just have a lot riding on this, that's all."

Nikki's last comment had Jorja turn to her with questioning eyes.

"What do you mean you have a lot riding on this?"

Now conscious that she might have said too much, Nikki quickly rebound with a lie.

"Don't look so surprised. I do still have a reputation to protect, you know. Having egg on your face when getting caught in the act is not fun and there's no way I'm going to go through that embarrassment again. Truce?" She stuck out her hand in gesture, but this time Jorja's instincts told her to ignore it.

"Sure, let's get the job done so we can both get on with our lives," she said instead.

But the atmosphere in the room was strained while they each worked in silence searching for the painting—and a way out.

"Nikki, can you hear me?" Harry's voice suddenly blared in their ears.

"We hear you, Harry. Thought we lost you, what happened?"

"You did. The entire system rebooted, possibly due to a routine server update. Good news is, while that happened, it caused vulnerabilities in their security and I managed to get into the system with a back door. No more timed windows, whoo-hoo!" he cheered.

"I have no idea what all of that means, but I'm happy to have you back in my ear. What can you tell us about this ice box we're in?" Nikki asked.

"You're in an ice box?"

"I don't know what we're trapped inside of, Harry, we just need to get that painting and find a way out."

"I've got nothing on my end, Nikki, but I'll keep looking," he reported.

As Nikki waited for Harry to hack them out of there, Jorja stood staring at a spot on the back wall. She reached inside one of the larger pockets of her cargo pants and pulled out a stethoscope, holding it up to wall covering small sections.

"Wow, not one of the tools we'd use nowadays, but okay. I guess old school might crack it today. Let me know when you find the heartbeat, will you?" Nikki's tone was sarcastic and mocking.

But Jorja didn't bite and continued to move the bell along the wall in front of her.

Now realizing she was clearly onto something, Nikki watched in silence as she worked. Before long, Jorja had moved her focus to the floor beneath her feet, squatting down to run her hands over the smooth, white surface. When Nikki could no longer stand her curiosity, she finally spoke.

"Are you going to let me in on what you're doing or not? You look like you've found something."

A smile broke across Jorja's face as she got up and moved to another section of the floor. Moments later she had her pocket-sized flashlight beaming onto the floor next to her feet, twisting the dial onto the blue-light feature.

"I knew it!" she exclaimed.

"What?" Nikki said, still not sure what Jorja found.

"See this, here? X marks the spot. These are pressure sensors, and, if I'm correct, it will reveal our painting. I need you to step on top of this mark at the same time as me, okay?"

Nikki nodded and Jorja counted them down.

Together they stepped atop the markings that were only visible under a blue light, and as they did so, something clicked in the wall in front of them. In an instant, a section in the wall released as a panel sprung open.

"Well, I'll never," Nikki said, open-mouthed.

When Jorja swung the panel open, they were greeted by a cavity in the wall, its sides lined with expensive cushioned red satin. And sitting in what looked to be crafted in pure gold, a cradle that held the painting they'd been searching for.

"You did it. You actually did it. I can't believe you found the *Salvator Mundi*." Nikki spoke with awe.

Mesmerized by its mystical beauty, elated that she had accomplished the impossible and found what was needed to buy back Ben's freedom, Jorja reached in and lifted the painting from its cradle.

But, as she expressed her gratitude to God from deep within her heart, a piercing alarm echoed through the white, empty space around them. A bolt system snapped in place from inside the door behind them, causing them to spin around at the same time. Above their heads, a vent whirred open followed by three beeping sounds that were barely audible over the piercing sounds of the alarm.

And as they stared up into the roof, their loot in hand, white clouds of gas bellowed from inside the vent.

CHAPTER THIRTY-ONE

F ear gripped at their insides as the once notorious
pair of master thieves stood gaping at the steady flow
of gas swirling above their heads. Nikki ran toward the
door, slamming into it with her shoulder.

"Harry! Get us out of here! We're about to be gassed to
death!" Nikki shouted.

"I'm trying, the door was triggered remotely and runs
independently from the server, a fail-safe of sorts."

When Nikki turned around, she found Jorja on her
knees where she had already opened the back of the
painting and was now carefully rolling the antique canvass
into a scroll. After tucking it inside her jacket, she ripped
the satin cloth from inside the walls of the safe and tore
two large strips out of it.

"Here, cover your face."

Nikki did as instructed while she observed Jorja, who had

now moved to the wall next to her. Once more she placed the stethoscope bell against the wall, pausing briefly as she listened, then quickly stepped back into the farthest corner.

"You might want to join me, it's about to blow," she cautioned Nikki who didn't hesitate to react.

Moments later her heed proved true and from beyond the snowflake-like white debris that filled what was left of the tiny room, Mo's tattooed face emerged.

"I got you ladies," he said, grinning like a Cheshire cat.

WHEN THEY HAD SAFELY MADE it through the gaping hole Mo had blasted into the vault room's wall, he led them down a short, dark, and narrow passageway that soon met up with a low-arched open doorway.

"Where did all this come from? I don't recall seeing it on the blueprints," Jorja queried.

"That's because no one knows of its existence," Mo replied as they turned right, ducking down to accommodate the low bricked roof.

"This, ladies, is the inside of the property's perimeter wall, and pretty soon, we will exit into the desert at the back of the property."

"How did you find this, Mo? I have to say, I am impressed," Nikki praised him.

"One doesn't spend four years in Iraq without picking up a thing or two on their neighbors. It's how they protected their territories in the old days, from within the walls. The good old Trojan horse."

"Now you're really showing off," Nikki laughed, her voice teasing.

Mo stopped and threw his backpack on the dusty ground as he knelt down beside it. They watched as he took out detonation cord and few sticks of dynamite.

"You're going to want to move back a tad, ladies. We're doing this cowboy style."

Hardly a minute later, the explosives easily blasted a hole through the wall and it wasn't long before they stepped out into the open desert that backed up to the sheik's property.

As the sky lit up in bright, glowing stars above her head and the moon illuminated the golden sand beneath her feet, Jorja gave thanks to the one who truly saved her.

Their feet hit the firm sand as they ran towards the dunes in the far distance until the sand became thick and loose beneath their feet.

"Kalihm, do you read me, over?" Mo called for him over a two-way radio.

"Reading you loud and clear, Mo, over."

"Mission accomplished, I repeat, mission accomplished. We're on our way to the extraction point, over."

"Copy that, Mo, well done. Your chariot awaits, over and out."

But, as soon as they dipped behind the next dune,

Nikki's voice cut through the thin air where she'd been trailing behind them.

"Hand it over," she said, causing both Jorja and Mo to spin around in surprise.

Stunned, neither reacted to her command.

"Come on, I don't have all night. Hand over the painting, Jorja."

"Why, where's Pascale? It wasn't part of our deal," Jorja replied which had Nikki laugh out loud.

"You stupid woman. Like I said earlier, you have been out of the game for too long. The rules of the game have changed and I win." She held out her open hand.

"Nikki, what are you doing? Put down the gun," Mo urged, confusion spread thick on his face as well.

"It was fun while it lasted, Mo. We could have been good together."

"What are you talking about, Nikki? Our extraction point is just over the next dune. Lower the gun and let's go."

"Our paths end here, Mo darling. Like I said, we could have been good together. But you had made it very clear you only play by the rules, so, here we are, at the end of the road."

"Where's Pascale?" Jorja cut in.

"Who cares? By the time he finds out he's been played, I'll be long gone. With the painting. Now stop messing around and hand over the painting, or I'll kill you both."

She pulled her thumb back on the gun's hammer, signaling she meant what she had said.

Mo charged toward her, his face red and his eyes glowing.

"Not if I kill you first, you lying—"

A single gunshot echoed through the air before Mo tumbled to his knees, blood staining his pants over his outer thigh.

"You shot me, you actually shot me," he groaned.

"That one was to stop you, the next one is going to kill you if you try something like that again."

"Not on my watch, Nikki, drop your gun!" Pascale's voice suddenly cut in behind her, his sides flanked by a dozen armed men.

Elation soon faded and made space for pain instead as Jorja scanned their uniforms, all of which—including Pascale's—were marked with bold white letters that told her they were Interpol. Feeling instantly ill and filled with dread, Jorja watched the scene play off in front of her.

"I said, drop your gun, Nikki!" Pascale repeated while Jorja's mind scrambled to put the pieces together.

Pascale's face was stern, his gun aimed directly at Nikki while his eyes were focused entirely on the gun she now dropped at her feet as she turned around to face him.

"How long have you known?" Nikki asked Pascale as his Interpol team arrested her.

"Since the moment we brought you onboard. As the saying goes, once a thief, always a thief."

As the words left his mouth his gaze briefly met Jorja's, her eyes filled with sadness caused by the bitter sting of his betrayal and the words he'd just spoken.

But what hurt most was the truth that lay at the very core of his words. She had been in denial, all this time pretending she was someone she wasn't, when all she'd been was a thief, a despicable being who could never change.

Tearing her gaze from his, her insides crushed by the fact that her worst fears had come true, she let his men take the painting from her before they bound her hands in cuffs as well.

It was all over. Her instincts had been correct all along. Pascale Lupin had played her, played with her heart and with her future.

And trusting him had cost her everything.

THANK you for reading SHADOW OF FEAR! Are you still breathing? Good, you're going to need to hold on tight with book 3!

Jorja faces the ultimate test when her treacherous journey continues in the **final installment, WAGES OF SIN.**

But will she realize in time that the life she thinks she's always wanted might not be the same as the one God conceived?

Or will she end up losing it all?
One-click Wages of Sin now!

"Book 3 begins in fifth gear, connecting with the ending of Book 2, with no letting up of adrenaline pumping until the end of the book. Yes, this book is a thriller. Urcelia has fully utilized her incredible creativity in this book. So many unexpected twists and turns. A rather incredible ending, where all of the loose ends are neatly tied up. The book kept me on the edge of my seat. It is a definite page turner. (I hated having to turn off the light at night....)"

BOOK 3: It all comes down to this!

The last installment of the Valley of Death trilogy races at a rip-roaring pace to a tense ending!

After risking life and limb to save Ben in Shadow of Fear (book II), Jorja walks straight into a trap she didn't see coming. Hopeless, her faith wavering, and with no way out, she does the unthinkable to survive, all in the name of freedom.

But freedom comes at a price and terror and betrayal are mild compared to what's coming.

Read on to see how the story ends!

I appreciate your help in spreading the word, including telling a friend. Reviews help readers find books! Please leave a review on your favorite book site.

You can also visit my online store (https://shop.urcelia.com)for exclusive discounts, merchandise, and promotions on my books.

Turn the page for an excerpt from WAGES OF SIN.

EXCERPT FROM WAGES OF SIN - BOOK III

WAGES OF SIN

(Book 3 in this series)

CHAPTER ONE

Jorja sat alone in the quiet room inside the British Consulate in Abu Dhabi. She no longer felt any emotions, nor did she know if she ever will again.

Numbed by the unexpected turn of events, and mourning Ben, whom she was certain Sokolov had already killed by now, she stared at the disposable cup of cold coffee they had posted in front of her hours ago.

She had not seen or heard from Pascale since his men took her away and locked her inside the room, and she had long since given up on thinking that she'd walk out of there a free woman.

From where she sat in the middle of the small room, staring out of the tiny rectangular window at the very top of the wall, she watched the sun's rays grow brighter as it announced the start of the new day. It had been days since she slept, not that she cared much any longer. Nothing mattered anymore. Everyone she had ever loved and cared for had been stripped away from her, even the person she once was.

She had tried talking to God, searching for answers, the truth. But instead, she had found her heart hardened and her spirit angry with Him. She had thought that she could trust Him, that He was helping her. But even that wasn't to be.

Her mind trailed to the words she had clung to before it all began, but this time, it brought her nothing but pain. She had been in a valley of the shadow of death, feared evil, faced it head-on, remained in its cold grip, yet she could not sense God anywhere.

Had He forsaken her because she had sinned? Perhaps she was wrong to think He should help her in the first place. Whatever it was, it was clear.

She would pay for her sins for the rest of her days.

Caught up in her agony, her mind trapped in another dimension, she jumped when the door suddenly shut beside her. When she turned to find the person who had entered, she saw that it was one of the officials who had briefly popped in to drop off her luggage. She had left it at the hotel in Geneva. How was it that they had found it? Why was it there?

Her heart bolted as a million questions ran through her mind and she recalled the files she had hidden inside. She shot across the floor to pick up her suitcase, lifted it atop the desk and moved to open it.

"Don't bother, it's not there anymore."

Pascale was suddenly behind her, his face warm and inviting like the day she had sat next to him on the plane.

"I don't know what you're talking about," she lied, her heart guarded.

"Take a seat, Jorja. We have a lot to discuss."

"I have nothing to say to you."

"Oh, I'm sure you do, but even if I believed that, there is a lot I have to say to you. So, please, sit down."

She did, watching him move the suitcase back onto the floor before he sat down opposite her.

"I want legal representation. I've been asking for one since you brought me here. I know my rights. You can't keep me here."

"You won't need one if you cooperate with us."

"Cooperate with you? And do what exactly? You already got what you wanted, so what's left? I'll tell you what's left, the bitter taste of betrayal."

She crossed her arms and stared blankly out the small window.

"Fair enough, you have every right to be angry. But I have a right to explain my side also."

"No, you don't. Nothing you can say will fix this, Pascale. You played me, used me, and now Ben is dead. And it's all thanks to you. We had a deal and you didn't honor it. But I guess you knew you weren't going to right from the start. So, I guess the joke's on me."

Pascale didn't argue, instead his fingers tapped at his mobile, holding it up for her to watch something on the screen.

When she looked she saw Ben, his face badly beaten, his voice strained when he spoke.

"Jorja, it's me. I'm told you're okay. I'm fine too. I knew you could do it. Then again, you learned from the best." He laughed then flinched when his smile pulled at a wound on his lips. "Anyway, I can't wait to see you and hear all the details. Hopefully, that will be soon." He blew her a kiss before the video shut off.

Want to read more? <u>One-click Wages of Sin now!</u>

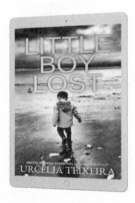

MORE BOOKS BY URCELIA TEIXEIRA

Angus Reid Mysteries series
Jacob's Well
Daniel's Oil
Caleb's Cross

Adam Cross series
Every Good Gift
Every Good Plan
Every Good Work

Jorja Rose trilogy
Vengeance is Mine
Shadow of Fear
Wages of Sin

Alex Hunt series
The Papua Incident (FREE!)
The Rhapta Key
The Gilded Treason
The Alpha Strain
The Dauphin Deception
The Bari Bones
The Caiaphas Code

PICK A BUNDLE FOR MASSIVE SAVINGS exclusive to my online store!
Save up to 50% off plus get an additional 10% discount coupon.
Visit https://shop.urcelia.com

More books coming soon! Sign up to my newsletter to be notified of new releases, giveaways and pre-release specials.

MESSAGE FROM THE AUTHOR

All glory be to the Lord, my God who breathed every word through me onto these pages.

I have put my words in your mouth and
covered you with the shadow of My hand
Isaiah 51:16

It is my sincere prayer that you not only enjoyed the story, but drew courage, inspiration, and hope from it, just as I did while writing it. Thank you sincerely, for reading *Shadow of Fear*.

I appreciate your help in spreading the word, including telling a friend. Reviews help readers find books! Please leave a review on your favorite book site.

MESSAGE FROM THE AUTHOR

Writing without distractions is a never-ending challenge. With a house full of boys, there's never a dull moment (or a quiet one!)

So I close myself off and shut the world out by popping in my earphones.

Here's what I listened to while I wrote *Shadow of Fear*:

- 10 Hours/God's Heart Instrumental Worship—Soaking in His presence (https://youtu.be/Yltj6VKX7kU)
- 2 Hours Non-Stop Worship Songs—Daughter of Zion (https://youtu.be/DKwcFiNe7xw)

When I finished writing the last sentence of the book!
How great is our God—Chris Tomlin (https://youtu.be/KBD18rsVJHk)

ABOUT THE AUTHOR

Award winning author of faith-filled Christian Suspense Thrillers that won't let you go!™

Urcelia Teixeira, writes gripping Christian mystery, thriller and suspense novels that will keep you on the edge of your seat! Firm in her Christian faith, all her books are free from profanity and unnecessary sexually suggestive scenes.

She made her writing debut in December 2017, kicking off her newly discovered author journey with her fast-paced archaeological adventure thriller novels that readers have described as 'Indiana Jones meets Lara Croft with a twist of Bourne.'

But, five novels in, and nearly eighteen months later, she had a spiritual re-awakening, and she wrote the sixth and final book in her Alex Hunt Adventure Thriller series. She now fondly refers to *The Caiaphas Code* as her redemption book. Her statement of faith. And although this series has reached multiple Amazon Bestseller lists, she took the bold step of following her true calling and switched to writing what honors her Creator: Christian Mystery and Suspense fiction.

The first book in her newly discovered genre went on to win the 2021 Illumination Awards Silver medal in the Christian Fiction category and the series reached multiple Amazon Bestseller lists!

While this success is a great honor and blessing, all glory goes to God alone who breathed every word through her!

A committed Christian for over twenty years, she now lives by the following mantra:

"I used to be a writer. Now I am a writer with a purpose!"

For more on Urcelia and her books, visit www.urcelia.com

To walk alongside her as she deepens her writing journey and walks with God, sign up to her Newsletter - https://newsletter.urcelia.com/signup

or

Follow her on

Facebook: https://www.facebook.com/urceliabooks

Twitter: https://twitter.com/UrceliaTeixeira

BookBub: https://www.bookbub.com/authors/urcelia-teixeira

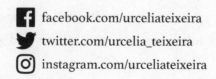

facebook.com/urceliateixeira

twitter.com/urcelia_teixeira

instagram.com/urceliateixeira

Made in the USA
Las Vegas, NV
27 February 2024

86419087R00163